The *HAZY FABLES* Middle-Grade Series

Hazy Fables Book #1: Hobgoblin and the Seven Stinkers of Rancidia

★Kirkus Reviews Best Books of 2019

★Foreword INDIES Book of the Year Award

★"Readers will giggle through every page
of this smart political satire."
—*Kirkus Reviews, starred review*

"Engages hard-to-please tween readers with
imaginative adventure…Read it together at bedtime to share
laughter and a positive message of empathy and inclusivity."
—*The Seattle Times*

Hazy Fables Book #2: Zombie, Or Not to Be

★Foreword INDIES Book of the Year Award Finalist

"Highly recommended…A pandemic, environmental issues,
and characters who do not believe in science are themes all too
suitable for students seeking contemporary fiction…Middle
graders hungry for the next zombie book will devour this one."
—*School Library Journal*

"A standing ovation for undead environmentalist theater."
—*Kirkus Reviews*

To my family, for the holiday spirit.
– K.S.

ISBN: 978-1-948931-26-7

First edition: September 2021
Published by Hazy Dell Press, LLC

Printed in China.

10 9 8 7 6 5 4 3 2 1

Find all Hazy Dell Press books at hazydellpress.com.

Krampus Confidential

Hazy Fables Book #3

by Kyle Sullivan   art by Derek Sullivan

HAZY DELL PRESS®
PORTLAND · SEATTLE

Cast of Characters

Marley

Ruprecht
[ROO-PREKT]

Nowell Rook

Frau Perchta
[FROW PERK-TAH]

Jóla
[YO-LAH]

Det. Metoh
[MEE-TOH]

Sgt. Schnee

Pickwick

"Rudy *the* **Remarkable"**

Grýla
[GREE-LAH]

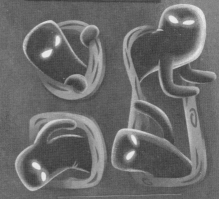

The **Yule Kids**

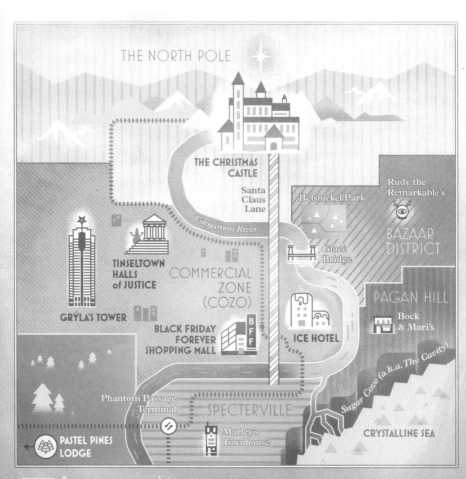

THE NORTH POLE

THE CHRISTMAS
CASTLE

Santa
Claus
Lane

Belsnickel Park

Rudy the
Remarkable's

BAZAAR
DISTRICT

Cinnamon River

Glacé
Bridge

TINSELTOWN
HALLS
of JUSTICE

COMMERCIAL
ZONE
(COZO)

PAGAN HILL

Bock
& Mari's

GRÝLA'S TOWER

BLACK FRIDAY
FOREVER
SHOPPING MALL

B
F
F

ICE HOTEL

Sugar Cove (a.k.a. The Cavity)

Phantom Passage
Terminal

SPECTERVILLE

CRYSTALLINE SEA

PASTEL PINES
LODGE

Marley's
Townhouse

Tinseltown
CAPITAL of YULETOPIA

Table of Contents

BORN ON THE NAUGHTY LIST

nce upon a time, it was midnight in Tinseltown. Not a creature was stirring on Hereafter Avenue, unless you counted me and my best friend, Marley. I'm a krampus and she's a ghost. Stop me if you've heard this one.

The crescent moon was a thin white scratch mark in a pitch-black sky. The night was frozen, the darkness heavy. Shadows brooded all around us, in the alleyways and along the edges of the narrow haunted townhouses lining the street.

It was December 5, also known as Krampus Night. In other parts of the city, Townies were out celebrating the holiday by brandishing birch branches and scaring the Christmas pudding out of each other in horned, toothy-grinned masks.

As an actual krampus, with real horns and fangs and the whole krampus shebang, I didn't need a mask to scare anyone. And, as an actual krampus, I wasn't sure how to feel about the holiday. Were they out there celebrating my species, or were they making fun of it?

Long ago, according to legend, krampuses would scare kids into nice behavior at this time of year. And it wasn't just my ancestors' looks that did the scaring. Krampuses were said to snatch naughty youngsters from their homes, shackle them in chains, and carry them away in baskets.

This may have been the case way back when, but today's parents would find this behavior inappropriate, to say the least. And anyway, it's not my idea of a good time. Not even the playacting version on Krampus Night.

No, this krampus was too busy to take part in the spooky hijinks of my species' honorary holiday. Tonight, this krampus had other plans.

Marley and I were about ten feet above Hereafter Avenue in Tinseltown's Specterville neighborhood. I was seven steps up on a ladder that leaned against the front of Marley's decaying, flat-faced townhouse.

Even with a full body of fur, a sweater, a jacket with an upturned collar, a woolen scarf, and a fluff-trimmed Santa hat, I still had to hunch my shoulders to ward off the torments of a subzero Tinseltown wind.

As a ghost, Marley doesn't have to worry about physical inconveniences like body temperature. Or like gravity, for another example. She was now floating at my side as we both guided a wooden sign onto black metal hooks. Not every ghost in Specterville can interact with the physical world, but Marley's been dead for 175 years. She's had some time to practice.

Marley was thirteen when she kicked it, so she'll be thirteen forever in the form of a gray, shimmery, semi-transparent spirit with white flowy hair and bright, pupilless eyes. As always, she wore a lacy blouse with flared sleeves and a long, pleated skirt that faded out of existence before it got to the place her feet should be.

With the sign in place and swaying in the wind, Marley and I exchanged nods.

I carefully stepped my hooves down the ice-slicked ladder. After a few strides into the crunchy, snow-packed street, I turned with a proud smile to read the sign—Krampus & Marley: Confidential Investigations.

The sign wasn't my best work, but it would do the trick. My usual woodworking tools were back up in the North Pole, where I'm from. But I did what I could using Marley's dad's tools, most of which were from an earlier century and more than a little rusty.

And while my first name is Ruprecht, I liked the authority of going by "Krampus" on the sign. Nobody knew who Ruprecht was, but everyone knew about krampuses.

Marley assessed the sign with arms crossed and head cocked. Her first name is Viviana, but she prefers to go by her last name, Marley. So that's what we call her.

"Not bad for a dead girl and a goat boy," she said with a smirk.

I pulled a miniature candy cane from my pocket and unwrapped the plastic. I popped the candy into my mouth and turned to respond. But before I could let loose a wisecrack, a heavy-duty blast of wind shoved me from behind. I steadied my hooves as the same gust whisked a small whirlwind of snow up from the ground to twist through the air before us.

The red, purple, and green holiday lights lining the town-house wobbled in the wind, as did the dramatic electric light

display that connected the rows of townhouses on both sides of Hereafter Avenue.

It was an intricate web of lights in the form of a black widow spider, with the spider's usual hourglass marking replaced with a holly sprig.

The wind was too strong. It ripped a line of lights off the building and knocked the black widow off balance. The spider billowed violently in the gust.

"I'd better wrangle that arachnid," sighed Marley. "Otherwise she might blow away somewhere and traumatize an elf."

Marley shot off into the night and left me alone on the ground. Suddenly, I became very aware of the darkness surrounding me. The shadows were everywhere. Wherever holiday lights didn't shine, darkness gazed back. I loved it down here in Tinseltown, but it was going to take some getting used to.

As Marley worked on the light display above, I peeked over

my shoulder to the northern skyline. There, atop snow-covered hills, and beneath a blazing North Star, the joyful, familiar lights of the Christmas Castle kept watch over the city.

I took a moment to take it in: the red-and-white-striped spires and turrets, the twinkling white lights, and the grand red doors at the center of the castle's festive and iconic exterior.

The Christmas Castle marks the beginning of the North Pole suburbs. And while both Tinseltown and the North Pole are in the country of Yuletopia, as far as I'm concerned, they might as well be in different galaxies.

Up there in the suburbs, things are sparkly and beautiful, but they're also a little more manicured and fenced in. A little more protected. In other words, a little more boring.

And that's a big reason why I was down here spending my winter break with Marley. I'm basically allergic to boredom.

I turned from the castle as Marley floated down from the black widow light display. She gave me a comically exaggerated look of exhaustion and pretended to wipe her forehead. Ghosts don't actually sweat.

"Whew!" she said, alighting by my side. "It took a couple of clove hitches to secure her, but I think the old girl will live to stalk another night."

"Nice work, Marley," I said, my teeth bearing down on the candy cane in my cheek. I rubbed my arms to stay warm.

"Want to head inside and let our sign do its thing?"

"I know you're freezing your tail off," said Marley. "But there's just one final touch to make sure we grab the attention of every down-on-their-luck Townie in Tinseltown."

Marley grabbed a string of white lights from the ground and floated up to the sign. As she framed the sign with the bright bulbs, she called down to me, "We're going to help out so many Townies, you'll never be blamed for anything again. Just wait and see."

It seemed like a long shot, but I hoped she was right. The main reason we'd started this detective agency was to help people, especially those who existed on the margins, like krampuses and ghosts. But we also wanted to help one krampus in particular: me.

By helping people fix their problems, we wanted to prove, once and for all, that I wasn't a bad kid.

The truth is, in the North Pole, I've been blamed for a lot of things. Most of which I didn't do. Throughout my childhood, whenever something went wrong—when a cookie was snatched, when a present was opened prematurely, when a toy broke, when a Christmas tree toppled over, when an icicle plunged from a rooftop—all eyes dashed to me.

I'd always assumed that I got blamed for things because I was different. The North Pole is a place of mostly elves, and as far as I know, I'm the only krampus who lives there. There are krampuses in the city—I've seen them myself—but up there, a kid like me sticks out like ink splattered on a snowman.

Mishaps trailed my hoofsteps wherever I went. At times it felt like I was being targeted because I was a krampus, and other times it felt like plain old bad luck. Maybe it was a little of both.

For a while, I was only blamed for little things, so I learned to live with it. But last year, I got blamed for a big thing, and everything changed.

It was a big enough thing that the cops got involved. Big enough that I was suspended from Jack M. Frost Middle School. Big enough to smear my reputation for keeps.

I was completely innocent, and my parents believed me. But the school didn't. And neither did the cops.

Don't get me wrong, I haven't been a saint my whole life. I've pulled my fair share of pranks on gullible elves. I've snuck out to go sledding at night. I've snooped for Christmas presents like a world-class cat burglar. Like most twelve-year-olds, I'm a little bit naughty and a little bit nice. But I'm no criminal.

And while most folks in the North Pole are tolerant and kind, some couldn't help but judge a kid like me. Some presumed my guilt even without evidence. And now they had evidence.

To them, I was a krampus and I'd always be suspect. To

them, I was born on the naughty list.

"You OK, Ruprecht?" Marley was back from stringing the lights. "You seem a little lost in your thoughts, even for you."

I became aware that I was twisting my candy cane in my mouth and once again staring off toward the Christmas Castle.

"I'm OK, Marley," I said with a small smile. "I guess I always get a little thoughtful on Krampus Night."

"Are you sure you don't want to get out there and scare some Townies?" Marley asked, nudging me with her elbow. "It might make you feel better to show those posers how it's done."

I laughed. "Not tonight, Marley. We're in the helping business now, remember?"

We went inside, leaving our sign rocking back and forth in the screeching wind. Our detective agency had officially opened. Now we just had to wait.

Our sign was out there inviting people to drop their problems off at our doorstep, inviting them to turn their problems into our problems. You might say we were asking for trouble.

I peeked out of Marley's front window for one more glance at the bright, comfortable North Pole lights. My family was there, sleeping soundly with sugarplums and all that. My family, including my loving, encouraging parents who trusted me enough to let me spend winter break—the full month of December—in Tinseltown.

And while they knew where I was, they didn't exactly know my plans. They didn't know about the detective agency. For now, I was going to keep that little holiday secret tucked way back under the tree.

I guess it's true what they say. 'Tis the season for surprises.

CHAPTER ONE

KRAMPUS & MARLEY

Ten days later, I sat on the edge of a musty old-timey desk in a musty old-timey study. The tip of a half-dead candy cane poked out of my mouth.

My tired eyes dragged across dusty furniture and overstuffed bookshelves, across side tables stacked with curious volumes of forgotten lore, and past a dismal fire barely bothering to stick around. My eyes stopped when they caught themselves glowing back through the window's reflection.

My head, as with the rest of my body, was covered in charcoal-black fur. Two goat ears jutted out on either side, as if craving attention. From my forehead, two spikes darted up like the sharp horns of an antelope. Beneath my horns, distrustful eyebrows rested above two deep, glowing ovals that burned yellowly in the shadow and blazed a devilish red when reflecting light. Under my eyes, dark bags advertised to the world that last night, like most nights, I'd had trouble sleeping. And on my head, between my ears and behind my horns, I wore a Santa hat.

All in all, as with all krampuses, I looked something like a yuletide devil.

I smiled and then glared, glowered, and grimaced in turn. I tried to see how the world saw me. Scary. Untrustworthy. Menacing. I couldn't see it.

Even when I stuck out my uncommonly long and forked tongue, all I could see was a decent kid who got too little sleep.

My eyes moved beyond my reflection to focus on evening snowflakes spinning furiously in a white, swirly riot. Behind me, my tail twitched mindlessly in the air. Its tip, a paintbrush tuft of fur, swayed gently in tempo to an unknowable rhythm.

BRRIIINNG! A brass servants' bell jingled with urgency on the wall, jolting me out of my trance. There hadn't been a servant in this house for over a century, but the bell still came in handy. It helped Marley warn me before dropping in so I didn't have a heart attack.

"Yes, Marley?" I asked the empty room.

I turned away from my reflection in time to see my best

friend appear in a whirl of gray mist, as if whooshing in on the dark winter wind. She didn't always appear in this misty way, but when she did, it was for dramatic effect.

When she fully materialized, she was sitting on the blood-red upholstered chair beside the fireplace. Like the faint fire flickering to her left, Marley's transparent ghostly form subtly shimmered and danced like gray vapor.

Her tousled hair flowed past her shoulders. Her large, pupilless eyes smoldered with a bright white light. She was leaning back with arms crossed in a self-satisfied sort of way. The smirk on her face and a large misplaced tendril of hair suggested excitement with a dash of mischief. Her expression stood in complete contrast to her father's portrait scowling above the fireplace.

His name is Jacob, but I call him Mr. Marley. The portrait was painted when he was alive. The way the Marleys tell it, he was stern and cruel during his lifetime. He's changed his tune since becoming a ghost, and now he spends his time convincing the living to treat one another with empathy and kindness. The lead up to Christmas is his busy time, so he's rarely around to supervise us. Which is just how we like it.

"Knock, knock," said Marley with a smile. I could trace some pent-up energy, as if she was wrestling back a secret before it popped out of her mouth.

"Who's there?" I played along.

"A terrified elf," she said.

I raised a furry eyebrow and adjusted the candy cane in my mouth. "A terrified elf who?"

"A terrified elf...who might just be our first customer!" Marley disappeared for a nanosecond, and then, in a flash, she reappeared, floating at my side. Her white eyes flared with excitement.

I took the candy cane out of my mouth and stared at her, blinking robotically, like an animatronic Santa. Marley smiled patiently as she bobbed up and down in midair.

Then it hit me. "We have a customer? An elf? Right now?"

"I think so!" she said with a laugh. "Elves don't tend to visit haunted houses for no reason. I didn't want to scare him out of his jingly shoes, so I didn't show myself...I just unlocked the door, opened it a crack, and then called down from the top of the stairs, 'Come on in! Make yourself comfortable and we'll be right down!' He's sitting on a sofa in the parlor right now. Despite my best efforts, he's still shaking like a leaf."

I was stunned. Our sign had swung outside for ten days with not so much as a nibble. I was beginning to think of our little detective agency as a pointless game, just a lark we could laugh about when school came back.

But now, there was an elf in Marley's parlor, and it was

suddenly very real. An actual elf with actual problems that we were actually supposed to solve.

"What kind of elf?" I asked.

Marley raised a finger in the air and then disappeared in a showy swirl of mist. I knew this move well. I'd seen it a thousand times. She was scanning the study's shelves to find a book that might hold the answer. For whatever supernatural reason, she moved faster when she was invisible.

Marley was a voracious reader who took any opportunity to spend time with a book. Over her decades as a ghost, Marley had devoured all the books in all the libraries of Tinseltown. So, she decided to expand her horizons by floating up to the North Pole and haunting our libraries for a while. That's how we met two years ago, in the library of Jack M. Frost Middle School.

We hit it off immediately. She had read all about krampuses and was able to fill me in on facts and lore about my species that even I didn't know.

On top of bonding over all things krampus, we connected over countless stacks of science fiction, ghost stories, and most of all, detective stories. We loved the hardboiled ones the best, the lightning-paced ones filled with mystery and wit. We loved how the detectives usually came out on top, against all odds and no matter what scary, incredible, and fantastic characters they met along the way.

In detective stories, there were good characters and bad characters, sure, but there were also in-between characters. The detectives were heroic, but not always perfect. They had their flaws, like all of us. But rough edges and all, they were heroes because they spent their time helping people figure things out. They didn't always catch the wrongdoer, but they uncovered the truth. And, at my age, that sounded like a wonderful thing. I still had a lot of truth to uncover.

A large leather-bound green volume slipped off its shelf and hovered in midair. I heard Marley blow on it, sending a gray puff of dust billowing across the study. "*Elfipedia: A Modern Field Guide to Modern Elves, 36th Edition,*" said Marley's

disembodied voice.

I hopped off the desk, the book rested in my place, and Marley appeared by my side.

I watched as she flipped the pages to the "T" section and read aloud the alphabetical categories.

"Tawny elves…thunder elves…Tolkien elves…

tomten…ah! Here we go—tree elves." Marley ran her finger down a column of little thumbnail pictures that showed various types of trees paired with various types of elves.

Tree elves are one of the larger subgroups of elf. Almost every tree has a corresponding elf specifically suited to its size, shape, smell, and other characteristics.

"He's definitely in the evergreen category…" said Marley, her eyes darting across the page. Her finger stopped on a little elf grinning beside a ponderosa pine.

"This is it! He's a tree elf of the ponderosa variety. He's got the same leafy golden hair, the same ear shape, the same curled, pointy green shoes with little bells. He even has the same adorable belt made of baby pinecones."

Marley's celebratory smile disappeared when she saw my expression. I wasn't quite as ready to cheer. Not yet.

"We don't have to do this," she said, and I knew she meant it. "I can just scare him away and that will be that."

I wasn't scared, exactly, but I also couldn't ignore the tinge of anxiety in my stomach. It never occurred to me that our first client—so far, our only client—would be an elf. I guess I'd imagined we'd be helping someone more like me. Someone with hooves or horns or scales or talons. Someone who was misunderstood and wrongly judged by society, like me.

But that elf was likely in serious trouble. He wouldn't be in

Specterville if he wasn't. While everyone is at least a little bit afraid of ghosts, elves are positively terrified of them. Typically, elves avoid Specterville like snowpeople avoid saunas. This elf could be desperate, and we could be his only shot.

I jammed the candy cane back into my mouth and gritted my molars against it. "Let's shoo the elf upstairs, Marley," I said, heading to the door. "We hung the sign—the least we can do is hear him out."

Marley whirled around in a tight, excited circle in front of me. "Ooo! We're going to crack this case like a walnut!" she said, spectral teeth clenched with anticipation.

"You better wait here, though," I said. "Or at least go invisible. It sounds like the elf is already petrified. We don't want him fainting on us."

Marley smiled at me. "OK," she said. "But you're not exactly a snow angel yourself, you know."

"Point taken," I said. "I'll be sure to smile without teeth."

CHAPTER TWO

THE SHAKEN ELF

A s gently as I could, I coaxed the elf upstairs and into the study. He was now seated across from me on the other side of the desk. I breathed in and out and tried to look like a professional, though I was anything but.

The elf wasn't ready to spill his jelly beans quite yet, so I took him in in silence. As he sat there quaking, the room filled with the strong fragrance of ponderosas.

Two heads shorter than me, the elf wore various shades of green from the top of his pointy hat to the curled and bell-adorned tips of his shoes.

He was a dead ringer for the ponderosa elf from Marley's

book. Large protruding ears, leaflike golden locks of blond hair, even the belt of baby pinecones. On the chair beside him rested a backpack fashioned out of an acorn—a very big one, by acorn standards. Those nuts don't grow on evergreens, so he must have picked it up at a shop in the city.

I had my hooves up on the desk, trying to look casual and maybe put the elf at ease. I struck a match and reached over to light the three small candles in one of Marley's old-fashioned angel chime decorations.

The heat from the candles rotated a tin turbine at the top, which caused three tin angels to spin in a circle and strike bells beneath them: *Ting! Ting! Ting!* I didn't care for it much, but I knew the elf would like it. It might help him relax a little.

"Nog?" I asked. The Ghost of Christmas Present, a good friend of Mr. Marley's, visits often and keeps the pantry and icebox filled with food and goodies for living visitors like me. Feasting is kind of his thing, I guess.

Personally, I never touch eggnog. It's 95% sugar, and I have enough to deal with without adding a headache to the mix. The candy canes keep me edgy enough as it is.

"N-no, thank you," said the elf. He took off his felt hat and began torturing it in his lap. He gazed at me with large dark-brown bark-colored eyes. "I couldn't stomach it. I'm too upset."

I put my hooves on the ground and propped my elbows on

the desk. I knew this elf was scared, but elves never declined eggnog. While most elves were a little jumpy, this elf was shaken to his core.

Along with the chiming angels, I could hear the little bells on the ends of the elf's shoes jingle from his shaking.

"Ahh!" he screamed, and I flinched. Mouth agape, the elf reached a tiny finger and pointed over my left shoulder.

"A g-ghost...a girl g-ghost," he stammered.

Marley chuckled, and I turned around to shoot her a look. "I'd like to introduce my partner, Viviana Marley. You can call her Marley. She's a friendly ghost who sometimes forgets that not everyone is delighted to meet a spirit."

The elf hadn't stopped pointing.

"As I mentioned downstairs, my name's Ruprecht. And, my apologies, but I never did catch your name..." I prompted the elf.

"N-no..." The elf trailed off, eyes glued to Marley.

"No?" I asked, leaning back in my chair. "You want to remain anonymous?"

The elf gulped down a ball of fear the size of a Christmas ornament. "N-nowell. My name's Nowell Rook."

"Hello, Mr. Rook," I said. I tried to sound chipper, but it came out phony. "Now, what can we do for you?"

The elf didn't seem to hear me. He was still fixated on

Marley. "I-I'm sorry. I knew there'd be ghosts here, but it's very hard to concentrate."

The elf rubbed his arms and squeezed his eyes tight. "Y-you're giving me goosebumps."

Marley zipped out and floated beside the desk. The elf winced in fear. "OK, OK, I get it," she said, throwing her gray hands in the air. "This is going to be a thing. If I don't leave, this elf is never going to get his story out. I'll be downstairs practicing my organ."

"Thanks, Marley," I said. "Try not to take it personally."

With a huff, she disappeared in an indignant whirl of mist. It was now just me and the elf. He exhaled and looked slightly more comfortable. But only slightly.

"Now, let's try that again: what can I do for you, Mr. Rook?"

As nonthreateningly as possible, I laced my clawed fingers together on top of the desk. I tried to smile with my eyes. The edges of my mouth curled up to suggest friendliness, but not so much that my fangs showed.

The elf opened his mouth to speak, but then snapped it shut and shuddered as the deep moans of Marley's organ music vibrated up through the floor. The effect was very creepy, and I usually liked it creepy. But it wasn't doing the elf's nerves any favors.

"Never mind that," I said. "It's just a little mood music. Now, listen, Mr. Rook. You came to a doorstep in the haunted part of town with the words 'Krampus and Marley: Confidential Investigations' on a sign out front. You had a pretty good idea of what you were getting into, and now you're getting into it. So, please, tell me: what can I do for you?"

The elf put his hat back on and took a deep breath. As he spoke, his eyes wandered everywhere they could to avoid contact with my own.

"I'm sorry," he said, with a steadying breath. "As I mentioned, my name is Nowell Rook. I'm from a ponderosa pine tree in the Treacly Forest. My brother is from the same tree. His name is Tonttu, and he's a very naughty elf."

I reached for a musty and yellowed pad of paper, dipped an antique nib pen in ink, and jotted down the elf's details.

With a wheezy sigh, he twisted the cupped top of the acorn back-pack to open it, pulled out a photo, and held it up.

It showed a friendly looking tree elf with a

beaming smile that seemed to imply the opposite of naughtiness. It was a smile that appeared lighthearted and maybe a little naïve, but not naughty.

The elf must have noted my quizzical expression. He looked at the picture and said, "He doesn't look naughty, I know. But trust me—he's naughtier than a mogwai after a midnight snack. He's been naughty his whole life, but I'm afraid now he's gone too far. I think my brother is in with some bad characters… some *non-elves*."

I didn't like the way he said "non-elves." It had a whiff of prejudice.

I walked around the desk and took the photo from his quivering grasp. The pictured elf didn't look naughty, but then again, what good were appearances? With my horns and tail and teeth and claws, everyone assumed I was a naughty creature, even though I wasn't. Most of the time.

I handed the picture back to the elf and returned to my chair. "What exactly would you like me to do about it? I'm an amateur detective, not a life coach."

The elf placed the picture back in his acorn. "There was scuttlebutt in the forest that my brother, Tonttu, had moved to the city and gone full-on naughty. So, I traveled into Tinseltown and began trailing him. A few days ago, I saw him outside an abandoned ribbon-candy factory in Sugar Cove."

I jotted this down and made a side note to look up the word "scuttlebutt." I knew that Sugar Cove was a Tinseltown district east of Specterville. Popularly known as the Cavity, Sugar Cove was filled with candy factories and gingerbread mills surrounding a harbor that opened up to the Crystalline Sea.

"I saw him there," the elf continued. He tried to cover his face with one of his tiny elf hands. He seemed to struggle with this part of the story. "He was…speaking with a…a krampus."

The elf peeked through his fingers and studied my face, trying to note my reaction. I didn't give him one to note.

"Must run in the family," I said. "You also seem to have a thing for speaking to krampuses."

"What I overheard between the krampus and my brother made me sick," said the elf. "I was so upset, I just started walking and thinking. I was lost in thought and didn't notice I had wandered into Specterville. Then I looked up and saw a sign. Well, your sign, actually. I figured if anyone would know how to handle a situation involving a krampus, it would be another krampus."

"And tell me, Mr. Rook," I said, leaning forward in my chair. "What did you hear them talking about?"

The elf coughed, and his pupils danced nervously around the room. "I noticed your sign says *confidential* investigations," he said. "That means you won't tell anyone about this, right?

Not a single soul?"

"That's right," I said. "I promise I won't go caroling about this to anyone...except my investigative partner, Marley, of course."

The elf shivered at the mention of my deceased friend.

With a grim look, he nodded, and continued. "The krampus runs an underground candy operation, and he wants my brother to join. He's trying to flood the streets with unregulated peppermint bark. They're using a synthetic compound called buzzitrol that's ten times sweeter than sugar. The sugar rush it produces can be uncontrollable. They'll make a killing on the profits, but someone could get hurt."

"It sounds like what you need is a cop," I said, laying down my pen. "I can give you directions to the station."

"No way, I can't go to the cops," said the elf, his voice warbling with desperation. "Who knows what naughty, illegal things my brother's been up to? They'll toss him straight into the Cooler and lose the key."

"Jail isn't such a bad place for criminals, is it?" I asked innocently.

The elf sighed, causing his whole chest to heave. "You don't understand," he said. "My brother isn't like you. He isn't cut out for the city life with goblins and ghosts and krampuses. He doesn't belong with criminals. He belongs in the forest with simple things, like chipmunks and mushrooms and dewdrops."

The elf watched my response. I leaned further back in my chair.

"Please," he said, reaching his highest pitch yet. "I've tried so hard to reach him, but he ignores my letters."

I frowned at the elf. He responded with the largest, saddest elf eyes I'd ever seen. "He's an orphan, Ruprecht. We both are. If I don't help him—if you don't help me help him—he has no one else who will."

Crinkling the plastic on a candy cane, I searched for the right spot to tear it open. Was it possible this elf knew that I also started life as an orphan? Was it possible he was using this knowledge to soften me up? Either way, it may have been working.

I closed my eyes and my frown deepened. When I flicked my eyes back open, the elf recoiled.

"Even if I wanted to help, Mr. Rook, how would I find him? You're talking about a very small elf," I made a sweeping gesture toward the window with my candy cane, "and that's a great big city out there."

"After seeing your sign, I've spent the last few days racking my brain, trying to decide what to do. This morning, I came up with a plan. And I kicked the plan into motion by paying off a turtle dove to deliver one more letter to my brother."

"And what did the note say?" I asked. I put my hooves back up on the desk, first one, then the other.

"I admit it's naughty, but I lied to him." The elf dropped his eyes in shame. "I didn't know what else to do. I told him that I was a krampus who had come across several barrels of buzzitrol. I asked him to meet me on the Glacé Bridge. The one that crosses the Cinnamon River near the corner of Holly and Ivy. I said I'd give him an excellent deal on the barrels, but that he couldn't tell anyone."

"And when did you ask your brother to meet this krampus?" I asked.

"Midnight, the night after tomorrow," he said with an apologetic tinge. "December 17."

"It's a minor quibble," I said, "but you could have asked first."

"Please, Ruprecht, I'm beyond desperate," said the elf, all weepy-eyed. He pulled a paper sack from his acorn and set it on the desk. "I'm sorry, I should have asked first, and I know it's short notice, but I'm willing to pay you 2,000 chestnuts if you go there and try to talk him into coming home."

From the sack he pulled a brick of cash and fanned it out. They were red, green, blue, and white bills with little pictures of famous figures—Frosty, Rudolph, Governor Lucia, those kinds of people. It was Yuletopia's currency, and I'd never seen so much of it at once.

I whistled and said, "That's a lot of chestnuts, Mr. Rook."

There were many missing pieces to this elf's story. Enough to fill a toy shed. But there was a chance that his story checked out and he really needed my help. And that small chance was a big reason why we'd started our detective agency in the first place.

"Alright, Mr. Rook," I said. "I'll take the job."

The elf slid the stack across the table.

It felt a little uncomfortable to accept money from someone in such a tight spot, but really, it would have felt stranger to decline the payment. Taking the chestnuts would make our arrangement a professional one. Plus, it showed that the elf was willing to invest in his story.

"Thank you," said the elf. "You're doing the right thing."

"And will you be joining us on our little intervention?" I asked. I wasn't psychic, but I knew the answer before he said it.

"No, no, no," he said. He looked scared that I'd even suggested it. "My brother would run away if he so much as heard a single jingle from my shoe."

"Fair enough, Mr. Rook," I said. "You are the paying customer, after all. But I will need to know how to get in touch, of course."

"Ah, yes, of course," he said. He fumbled around in his acorn, pulled out a card, and handed it to me. It had the logo of an ice cube with "The Ice Hotel" typed in fancy letters. On the back was the hotel's address and his room number already scribbled in. "You can reach me there. Room 651."

The elf hopped down from the chair and slipped his acorn onto his back. A thought seemed to enter his head. He glanced nervously at the study door and turned back to me. "Is she out there?"

Suddenly, Marley's head poked up into the room through the floor. Her eyes were like spotlights. Her smile was the size of a toboggan. "I'm right here!" she announced with enthusiasm.

The elf screamed like a horrified banshee and scampered out of the study, down the steps, and out of the house.

"You heard everything, didn't you?" I asked Marley.

"You know it," she said, as she floated her full self into the study. "I actually never left the room. The organ was a decoy—it can play by itself. One of the perks of a haunted house."

"There's something off about that elf," I said. "But I can't quite put my claw on it."

Marley grabbed the chestnut bills and flipped through them like a deck of cards. "His story might be fake, but these chestnuts are real enough. What are you going to spend it on?" she asked with a mischievous grin.

As a ghost, Marley doesn't care much for money. But she knows how much it matters to the living. Far too much, if you ask me.

"A truckful of candy canes?" she joked. "Better yet, a candy cane factory?"

"The money was unexpected," I said. "But at least now we know the elf isn't kidding around."

Marley's expression turned thoughtful. "He's not kidding around," she said. "But is he telling the truth?"

"I guess we'll find out in a couple nights," I said, a fidgety feeling in my stomach.

"I hope we know what we're doing," she said.

"I can promise you, Marley. I don't have a single solitary clue."

CHAPTER THREE

JOLLIFICATION IN THE FOG

Two days later and thirty minutes before midnight, we were headed to the Glacé Bridge. It was a nice night if you liked your ice denser than a hockey rink and your fog thicker than a wool sweater.

Marley and I did like it like that, so we decided to hoof it instead of hailing a sleigh or taking a bus. As I walked and she floated, the only sound came from my hooves cracking through the iced-over snow.

For the past couple days, we had worked into the wee hours poring over books from the Marleys' heaving collection. As I crushed through an entire box of candy canes, we learned more than we'd ever thought possible about ponderosa elves, family interventions, Sugar Cove, peppermint bark, and the Yuletopia Food & Candy Administration's warnings about the frightening effects of buzzitrol on the brain.

Now that my head was full, it was time to use my hooves and my eyes. There was only so much we could do to prepare before we did what we were paid to do: meet an elf on a bridge and convince him to ditch the criminal stuff.

As we reached the cobblestones of Santa Claus Lane, snowflakes fluttered down through the blurry night fog. This was Tinseltown's main drag, right in the heart of the Commercial Zone. Townies called it the CoZo for short.

With collar turned up and claws shoved into jacket pockets, I tried my best to merge into the night. It was easier for a krampus and a ghost to blend in on the streets of Tinseltown than in the North Pole, but I was still a kid. And this was late for a kid.

At least Marley could go invisible if needed. I was stuck out in the open, feeling as noticeable as Rudolph's glowing red nose.

But luckily for us, the city was mostly asleep at this hour. The stores were closed up and resting after a busy day smack in the middle of holiday shopping season.

Every now and then the occasional car, sleigh, or snowmobile would jingle on by. When anyone passed on foot (or flipper or hoof or paw), I would duck my head down further and Marley would blink out of sight.

After twenty minutes, we had only passed a clawful of creatures: a penguin, two reindeer, a gnome, and a human. All of them seemed too tired or consumed by thought to notice us or anyone else.

Here and there, yellow candlelight illuminated rectangular windows in apartments above the boutiques and shops lining both sides of the street. A few windows glimmered with the faint flicker of hearth fires. Others were framed with frisky multicolored holiday lights that held vigil all night, perhaps in an attempt to drive away the dark spirits of winter.

The lights tried their best to add brightness and warmth to the dim, frigid night. But lights also create shadows. They can't help themselves. And tonight, despite mostly deserted streets, every shadow seemed alive. I kept catching movement in my peripheral vision, but when I'd crank my neck to look, there was nothing there. Just lights and shadows.

Ahead of us on the street corner, a trio of malamutes warmed their paws over a fire-filled barrel. Holiday piano music tinkled out of a boom box jammed into a nearby snowbank.

A twitchy movement to my left stopped me in my tracks. I jerked my head to look down a gloomy alleyway, but it was just fire escapes and darkness.

The music had stopped—the dogs sensed it too. They all

had their noses raised, probing the air with quick sniffs.

"There's something there," Marley whispered, peering into the alley.

As if waiting for the perfect cue, a black shape peeled off the shadow of a street lamp near the alley's entrance. Two of the dogs growled, one of them whined. The shape loosely resembled a small human. White eyes blinked into existence, looked at us, and narrowed. Then, at once, the shape shot away so quickly that I actually flinched.

Marley didn't have to say what she said next, but she said it anyway: "*Yule Kids.*"

And one Yule Kid was terrifying enough, but it was never just one. They always traveled together in their full pack of thirteen.

Everywhere we looked, dark shapes detached from larger shadows, elongated, and snapped open their piercing white eyes. On both sides of us, shadowy forms emerged from the darkness to glide out of sight along the sides of buildings and down Santa Claus Lane.

Marley and I stopped on the sidewalk and watched them soar away. When several shadows slipped past us from behind, I made the mistake of turning my head to look back.

Like rampaging ink blots, a swarm of Yule Kids dashed toward us. One of them pulled my hat off, zipped it up into the air above me, and flung it away.

The dogs had seen enough. They dropped down on all fours and booked it in the opposite direction. That seemed like a good idea.

"Let's get out of here!" Marley yelled. I ran down the sidewalk, picked up my hat, and darted into an alley. Marley rushed in front of me and stopped next to an open bright red dumpster. "Get in!" she yelled.

I clambered up the side and dove into a pile of discarded wrapping paper, ribbons, and packing peanuts. Marley slammed the lid over us as I crouched down. She stood up and stuck her head through the top of the dumpster like a periscope.

After a few seconds, she ducked her head back down. "They sure seem determined. They just whizzed on by heading northeast, like they had somewhere to be."

I unwrapped a candy cane and tossed the wrapper in among the garbage. "I wonder what Grýla has them up to in the CoZo."

Grýla is one of Tinseltown's meanest, most powerful witches. She runs a corporation called Illur Enterprises and uses her platoon of creeping shadows, the Yule Kids, to terrorize Tinseltown and do her bidding.

Nobody has been able to explain to me exactly what Illur Enterprises does, but it's clearly made its owner a ton of chestnuts. And, according to rumors, it does so in ways that

are not precisely legal.

"At the rate they're going," said Marley, "they'll be out of the CoZo in no time and into the Bazaar District."

"What could they want in the Bazaar District?" I asked. "I assume they're not ones for last-minute Christmas shopping."

"Maybe they're not headed to the CoZo or the Bazaar District…" Marley mused. Her eyes widened as we both reached the same thought.

"Maybe they're headed in between," I said. "To the Glacé Bridge."

My body filled with adrenaline at the thought of Grýla and the Yule Kids involving themselves in this buzzitrol business. It made sense that if there was a buck to be made illegally in Tinseltown, Grýla would want her cut. But who tipped her off?

There was no time for hypothetical questions—that tree elf might be in danger. I flung the lid open, jumped out of the dumpster, and sprinted after the shadows. Marley floated by my side.

My hooves crunched rapidly through the icy snow as we took a right onto Holly Street. Where Holly intersected with Ivy, we found the shiny silver Glacé Bridge stretching across the churning Cinnamon River.

The footbridge was strung up by thin wires decked with a white glaze that resembled icing. The bridge's footpath was made of transparent glass to showcase the rushing copper waters beneath.

As we approached the bridge, we could see two figures facing each other above the riverbank on the opposite side. They were obscured by the thick fog, but I could see that one figure was tall, the other short. Yule Kids swirled in the fog above them.

The two figures stood behind a red-and-white-striped fence that protected people and sleighs from rolling down the embankment and into the fast-moving water.

Yule Kids swarmed in and out of the fog, but they looked hesitant and uncertain. They seemed afraid, and as we got closer, I could see why. The sight stopped me in my tracks in the middle of the bridge.

One of the individuals was Tonttu, our client's brother. The other was a krampus. And an angry-looking one at that.

Marley gasped. I couldn't breathe. What was a krampus doing here? We watched, frozen, unsure what to do.

I could only see snippets between peels of rolling fog, quick glimpses of hooves, horns, and a tail. When I caught sight of a devilish grin plastered across a long yellow-eyed face, I understood in that moment how others could find my species so terrifying. I had to admit, the creature left quite an impression.

With claws outstretched, the krampus was holding

something in front of the elf. The fog shifted, and I could see it for the first time: it was a snow globe. The elf gazed at it, head tilted and mesmerized. Even above the noise of the roaring cinnamon waters, we could hear the krampus speaking to the elf, but we couldn't hear what he was saying.

Then, at once, the elf teetered backward as if unconscious, toppled over the fence, and rolled limply down the embankment. The elf's body stopped a few inches from the water—a few inches that may have saved his life.

The krampus blared out a shrill, maniacal laugh and trotted off across the street toward the pine trees of Belsnickel Park. It wasn't a fun laugh—it was an out-of-control, nothing-to-lose kind of laugh. The krampus's trotting gait had a little bit of a hitch to it. Like it was limping, or injured.

When the krampus reached the park's tree line, something

was startled out of the darkness. It was a small rotund form in a wide-brimmed hat. With a squeal of fear, it bounced down the street and out of view.

"Was that a goblin?" Marley marveled.

"That was a goblin," I deadpanned.

POOF! The krampus was suddenly engulfed in a thick cloud of smoke, possibly sulfur. And with that, it was gone.

The Yule Kids stopped swarming and bobbed indecisively in midair. They looked at each other, their white eyes expressing confusion. From the looks of it, the floating shadows were as mystified by the disappearing krampus as we were.

Even with the Yule Kids sticking around, Marley and I had to check on that elf. And we had to do it fast. We rushed across the slick, icy bridge to the snow-covered embankment on the other side of the river. Peering down, we could see the elf was breathing.

Only feet from the bobbing Yule Kids, I assessed the best path down to the victim.

WEEEOOOWEEEAAAH! WEEEOOOWEEEAAAH!

Out of the blanketing fog came the deafening wail of a siren and red-and-green emergency lights. Behind us on the street, a boxy white cop car screeched to a halt, "TTPD" and a snowflake logo painted on its side.

The bright lights illuminated the fog around us. After a

moment's hesitation, the Yule Kids rushed away in all directions and out of sight, like a scattering nest of airborne cockroaches.

I looked at Marley and she grimaced. It was the Tinseltown Police Department. I didn't need bifocals to see that this didn't look good.

A hulking yeti in a trench coat and a fedora stood up out of the car and kept on standing. He shook his furry white head.

"Stop right there, buddy. We got a call that there was a krampus running around jollifying elves." He glanced at me and then down at the elf below. "And, well, here you are."

━━━ CHAPTER FOUR ━━━

GOOD COP, COLD COP

In a blink, a crowd formed. Elves, fairies, humans, snow-people, and creatures of all kinds were rousted out of their beds after the commotion had dashed away their holiday dreams.

From somewhere in the crowd, the sad notes of a saxophone moaned out "Silent Night." But this was a Tinseltown crime scene. It was anything but silent.

"Move it! Make room!" bellowed the yeti cop. Beside us, a couple of elf deputies were stringing up red, white, and green crime scene tape to keep out the crowd, and to preserve the assailant's hoofprints in the snow. With a twinge of dread, I saw that the prints looked an awful lot like my own.

And even worse, the tracks stopped at the beginning of the street where the snow turned to ice. The cops would have to take our word for it that the culprit had continued across the street before disappearing by the park in a poof of smoke.

The gawking crowd stepped back as the yeti corralled them with his humongous furry white mitts.

The elf victim was on a stretcher, a grim, unhinged smile plastered across his face. His eyes were wide open, each one blinking bright white in alternating turns.

A snowshoe-hare medic waved coal under his nose in an attempt to revive him. The tree elf was alive, but it was going to take a few days before he'd be himself again. His headache would last for weeks, and his nightmares would last much longer than that.

"Before now, I'd only ever read about jollifications," said Marley, turning away from the victim's blinking eyes. "It's more disturbing than I ever could have imagined."

Elves live off holiday spirit. It's what gets them out of bed and puts a spring in their jingly step. However, elves can get so worked up that they become overexcited and actually overdose on holiday joy. Their systems crash and they fall into a deep coma-like trance. It's called jollification, and it isn't pretty.

In the North Pole, I'd seen elves accidentally jollify themselves before, especially in the run-up to Christmas. But those were minor cases. The elves just sniffed some coal, nursed a headache, and proceeded with caution. But this was something else. I'd never seen one this bad.

And I certainly had never seen a jollification committed against someone on purpose. The thought sent an icy tingle down my spine and through the tip of my tail.

Shaking my head, I unwrapped another candy cane. With the cane in my mouth and the wrapper in my pocket, I glanced over at the yeti. He was back at his squad car, growling into a two-way radio.

After arriving at the scene, he bluntly introduced himself as Detective Metoh and jotted down Marley's and my witness statements. The entire time, he kept his big white eyebrow hoisted with suspicion. And I could understand his skepticism—our story seemed unbelievable even to me, and I'd lived it. Yule Kids, a tree elf, a krampus, a snow globe, a jollification, a goblin, and a cloud of smoke. It was enough to make my furry head spin.

And while Marley and I told Detective Metoh the truth, we didn't tell him the whole truth. We honored our client's request for secrecy and left him, his brother's naughtiness, and the buzzitrol out of our story...for now. Eventually, I would tell the cops everything. But in the very least, I owed my client a warning before I started squawking.

A promise is a promise. Even in Tinseltown.

The medics wheeled the jollified elf past us and toward an ambulance painted with peppermint stripes. We heard the hare mutter to an elf cop, "Did you ID the victim?"

"Yeah, he had a passport on him. His name's Sprinkles," said the elf, thumbs tucked into his duty belt. "Cute name. Dreadful luck."

Marley and I exchanged scowls. Our client had lied to us about the victim's name. What else had he lied about?

"Krampus! Ghost! Get down here!" It was Detective Metoh again. He was down by the edge of the water where the elf had sprawled only minutes ago.

Through the fog, I walked and Marley floated down to the river. When we got close, we could see the yeti speaking to a narwhal who was peeking her head and six-foot-long tusk up from the cinnamon waters. It was a narwhal I knew.

"Hey, Mona," I said with a frown.

"Hey, Ruprecht," she said.

"You didn't mention that you two knew each other," said the yeti to the narwhal. His voice had an edge of suspicion. "That's quite the detail to leave out."

"I was getting there," said Mona. "I spend a lot of time in rivers and waterways that wind through the North Pole. I've known Ruprecht since he was a baby, and I can tell you he's not the krampus that committed this jollification."

"Family friend, hmm?" said the yeti as he jotted a note in his pad.

"Yes," said the narwhal. "But that doesn't change my story. Like I was saying: It was definitely a krampus who did the jollification—but not *this* krampus. He and the ghost came after the fact. The krampus who did it was taller, older looking. He used some kind of snow globe to do his dirty work. There were Yule Kids too, but they seemed to stick to the sidelines. They scrammed when you pulled up in the cop car. That's all I saw."

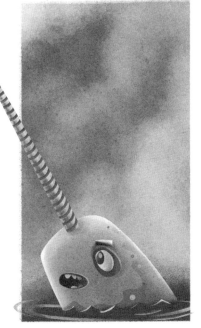

The yeti tossed a thumb toward me and Marley. "These two said the other krampus disappeared in a cloud of smoke by Belsnickel Park. Did you also see the other krampus poof into thin air?"

Mona gave me a look of apology. I gave her an encouraging smile.

"From my angle in the water, I couldn't see a cloud of smoke," said Mona. "But that doesn't mean it didn't happen."

Detective Metoh looked up from his notepad and gave the narwhal a probing stare. "Tell me, Mona," he said. "By any chance, did you happen to see a goblin?"

"A goblin?" Mona was taken off guard by the question. Just as Metoh wanted it. "No, why would I have seen a goblin?"

Mona looked at me and Marley, and her eyes dropped when she connected the dots. She bobbed up and down in the cinnamon waters. "Oh," she said. "Because they saw a goblin."

I turned to face Metoh. "So, Detective," I said, trying my best to adopt the wise-guy confidence of a seasoned private investigator. "We understand the elf's name is Sprinkles. Did you find any other clues? Where are we on determining a motive?"

"TTPD's finest are on the case," mumbled the yeti, absorbed and distracted by his notes. It sounded like a rehearsed non-answer that he might give to a beat reporter from the *Tinseltown Herald* or the HARK News Channel.

"Now listen up, kid," he barked, crouching down to my

level. He leaned in so that his bright blue face was only inches from my widening eyes.

"There aren't many krampuses in Tinseltown. Despite the coincidence, and the wild details to your story, I'm willing to see a version of reality in which you didn't jollify that elf. But there's no possible reality I can get behind in which you don't know more than you're letting on. If you weren't doing the jollification, what were you doing here? And don't forget: Withholding information from the TTPD can land you in far worse places than the naughty list."

"Like we told you," said Marley with a confidence I couldn't help but admire, "we were on Santa Claus Lane, the Yule Kids rushed past us, and we followed them here."

"That's the truth, Detective," I said. And it was, give or take a few details. "I'm a good kid, and so is Marley. It would never cross our minds to jollify anyone. You have to believe me."

The yeti sighed, but it turned into a growl before he finished. His knees popped loudly as he stood up from his crouch.

"All I got is the evidence, kid. I have no use for beliefs. They're based on feelings, not facts, and in the court of law, feelings are about as useful as a melted snowball."

"Excuse me, Detective, sir." Marley was wearing a cheesy grin that I think was supposed to look like innocence. "Is it OK if we go home now?"

"Sure, you can go home!" a voice roared down from the street. "But only if you don't mind riding in one of these!"

We looked up to see an ice troll grinning meanly down on us and banging on the hood of a TTPD squad car. She had a blast of white hair and blue skin covered in a thin layer of hoarfrost. It was Sergeant Schnee. I knew this ice troll, and she knew me.

Last year, when I was blamed for that big thing that got me suspended from school, Sergeant Schnee was the cop who showed up. She was convinced I was guilty, and recent circumstances would only make her all the more certain of my criminal nature.

The ice troll kept her eyes frozen on me. Marley floated up to my side for support.

"You heard the sergeant," said Metoh. "We're driving you two home."

Before heading up, I turned to Mona, who was watching me with sad eyes from the rushing water. "Goodnight, Mona," I said.

"Goodnight, Krampus," she said, a shade of fear in her voice. "And good luck."

The squad car's fog lights cut a streak in the night before us. The chained tires cracked and popped on the icy roads of downtown Tinseltown.

Behind the wheel, the yeti took up most of the front half of the car, with the ice troll squeezed into the passenger seat. Every so often, she'd turn back to stare me down cold. I stared back as innocently as I could, but it didn't seem to be working.

I met Schnee last year after someone had unleashed a poltergeist at the Jack M. Frost Middle School Christmas pageant. I was in the audience, just as shocked as everyone, as the invisible force flung hats, eyeglasses, scarves, and hand-bags into the air. It exploded overhead light bulbs and sent sandbags crashing down onto the stage. When it set off the fire sprinklers, everyone fled the auditorium in a soaked panic.

As it turns out, it's against the law to summon a poltergeist without a permit. The school received a tip that I was to blame, and my parents were called in. And, because a law was broken, the cops were called in, too.

When they searched my backpack and found a planchette for a spirit board—the exact type of planchette someone might use to conjure a poltergeist—my guilt was sealed in their eyes. Especially when they learned that my best friend was a ghost.

At the time, Schnee was working for the Illicit Conjurings division of Yuletopia's Inter-Veil Security Department. She's

the one who showed up to give me a ticket for illegally sum-
moning a Class-5 phantom.

As a minor, I avoided serious repercussions. But, along
with the ticket, I was suspended from school for a month and
required to de-ice the North Pole senior center every Saturday
for half a year.

But the worst consequence of getting unfairly blamed was
the distrust and suspicion I felt from many people, Schnee
very much included.

"So, tell me," she said, turned back in her seat and glaring.
"What's a tadpole like you doing on the city streets at midnight?"
Little blasts of frost pumped out of her nostrils as she breathed.

"Tadpole" was the insult of choice for Townies trying to
razz someone from the North Pole. She was trying to make
me feel like a suburban softy, but I wasn't going to let her get
under my fur.

I clenched my jaw, turned my gaze out the window, and
considered my options.

Holiday lights and ecstatic decorations zipped past us.
Metoh turned the car down an empty CoZo street lined with
closed-up shops. To our right, beyond spotlight beams criss-
crossing the skyline, the Christmas Castle shined regally above
the city.

Whatever it felt like to be there right now was probably the opposite of what I was feeling down here.

"It's not illegal to float down the street," said Marley. "We weren't harming anyone."

"Did you hear that, Metoh?" Schnee exclaimed with mock enthusiasm. She slapped Metoh's arm, causing him to grunt. "The ghost and the krampus weren't harming anyone!"

On a dime, she dropped the act, swinging around to deliver another furious glare. An icy breeze blasted through the car with her swift movement. Eyes squinted, she stared icicles at me.

"It's hard enough to trust a krampus on a good day," she sneered, "but it's especially hard when the krampus in question comes with a criminal record."

She turned back to face forward, shaking her head. "Did you know that poltergeist followed me home? Yeah, I bet you didn't know that. It didn't let me sleep for weeks. I had to burn a sleighful of sage to get it to leave me alone. You're lucky your parents helped you avoid doing time in the Cooler."

"Like I told you last year, I didn't release the poltergeist," I said. "Someone planted that planchette in my backpack."

Schnee snorted. "Right. Just like you didn't jollify that elf. For an innocent krampus, you sure seem to get yourself into some very guilty-looking situations."

Metoh peered at me through the rearview mirror. "Schnee's right, Ruprecht. We have a jollified elf in recovery at Saint Nikolas General Hospital. We have witnesses, including the phone call that tipped us off, that name a krampus as the jollifier. You are a krampus, and your hoofprints are all over the crime scene. It just doesn't look good, kid."

Metoh turned left. We were headed southbound on the outskirts of Specterville. The bright multicolored lights gave way to dull red, purple, and green lights on grimy brick houses. On the rooftops, snow laid plump and neat like thick tailored comforters.

When I didn't respond, Metoh added, "Just tell us what you're hiding. Tell us what you know and we'll cross you right off our naughty list."

I looked at Marley, who gave me an uncertain grimace to show that she was as undecided as I was. If I told the cops the truth, I would betray my promise to my client. But if I didn't tell the truth, I could end up in the Cooler.

With a sigh, I returned my eyes to the window. I couldn't break my promise, no matter how bad it looked. I at least owed the elf a chat. As soon as the cops left us alone, that's exactly what we would do. But for now, I had a freezing cold problem in the seat in front of me.

"Let me get this straight," growled Schnee. "You and the ghost are just taking a midnight stroll when all of a sudden a bunch of Yule Kids lead you to a jollification in progress. A krampus is there jollifying an elf with a snow globe, and then, out of nowhere, a goblin pops up, too. Are you sure you're not leaving anything out? Are you sure the Grinch didn't make an appearance?"

Marley and I didn't take the bait.

"Any thoughts on how the Yule Kids are connected to this?" asked Metoh. He adopted a pleasant tone, possibly in an attempt to balance out his partner's anger.

"Not a clue," I said.

"No idea," said Marley.

"You should ask Grýla yourself," I suggested. "Her tower isn't hard to find. Oh, look—there it is now."

To our right, high above the west side of Tinseltown, Grýla's skyscraper stretched menacingly into the night sky. Made of rust-red granite and glass, it served as the corporate headquarters for Illur Enterprises, and it was by far the city's tallest and most imposing structure.

"And what do you know about the victim?" asked Schnee. She was very committed to her list of questions. "Where is he from? Was he staying in Tinseltown? Was he staying at a hotel?"

"I've never met that elf before," I said. "Jollified or not."

"Do you own any snow globes?" asked Metoh. His tone suggested that it was the most innocent question ever asked.

"Of course," I replied, matching his tone. My answer made their eyes get big. "Relax, officers. I have one in my bedroom in the North Pole. Every kid in Yuletopia owns a snow globe."

"You sure you didn't bring it with you?" barked Schnee. "You sure you didn't toss it into the river after you jollified that elf?"

"We had nothing to do with this," said Marley.

"We're just doing our jobs," said the yeti. "We're trying to piece this together, and you two seem to be keeping secrets."

"No offense," I said, "but if you're pegging us as jollifiers, then you're piecing together the wrong puzzle."

We sat in silence as Metoh crackled up along the street and stopped the car in front of Marley's townhouse.

"Your dad home, Marley?" asked Metoh. "We'd like to talk to him."

"Nope," said Marley. "He's out of town. It's his busy season."

"That's fine," said Metoh. "We're more interested in talking to Ruprecht's parents anyway." He looked at me in the rearview mirror. "No matter how busy they are."

"Hey, Metoh," said Schnee, leaning forward and pointing through the windshield. "Get a load of that sign."

"'Krampus and Marley, Confidential Investigations,'" Metoh read with a stagey flourish. "That is a very interesting sign, Schnee."

Metoh's eyes once again filled the rearview mirror. "You've started a little detective agency, have you? And a *confidential* one at that?"

"It's nothing to worry about, Metoh," I said. "We're just doing what we can to support the community during winter break."

"Right," scoffed Schnee. "In the same way you supported that Christmas pageant at your middle school."

"You better tread carefully here, Ruprecht." The yeti sounded calm, but he didn't sound happy. "A krampus has jollified an elf, and right now, you're the only suspect."

"We'll be watching," said Schnee, eyeing me up and down. "And you better believe we'll be in touch."

Metoh pushed a button and the car doors unlocked with a *click*. My throat was made of chalk as we exited the cop car.

Slowly, with fake calm, we made our way up the steps to Marley's front door.

We went inside, locked the iron door behind us, and listened to the squad car's tires crunching along the ice. Neither of us said a word until the sound had completely died away.

CHAPTER FIVE

THE GREEN-EYED SHADOW

The next morning, I lay staring at the top of the four-poster bed that the Marleys had put me up in. As dull gray light gradually filled the room, I wondered if I had ever fallen asleep. All night long, awake or not, my mind never stopped spinning.

This whole situation was stuffed the wrong way up the chimney, and our client needed to help us unstuff it. We knew he had lied about the victim's name. What else had he twisted?

That question had company, a whole mob of them making a racket in my mind: Why would a krampus jollify an elf? Was he getting revenge on the elf for keeping secrets? What kind of snow globe could jollify like that? What was the krampus saying to his victim just before the jollification? What was the goblin doing there? And what about the Yule Kids?

With two baggy eyes, one aching head, and zero answers, I clomped downstairs. Marley and I needed to pay a visit to our one and only client, but first, unlike Marley, I needed to eat.

I swigged a mug of cider and wolfed down some roast beast cold cuts, courtesy of the Ghost of Christmas Present.

Feeling nourished if not fully rested, I threw on my sweater, jacket, scarf, and Santa hat. Marley blasted through the front door as if it wasn't there. I followed by opening the door to the streets of Tinseltown.

The city said "good morning" with a blast of icy wind. As I adjusted my Santa hat so it wouldn't blow away, I felt the hair on the back of my neck get all spiky. Someone, somewhere, was watching me.

Maybe the case was getting to me, or the suspicious cops had made me paranoid, but I couldn't shake the eerie feeling that comes with stalking eyes.

We took a slight detour northeastward into the Pagan Hill neighborhood so I could restock my supply of candy canes. Bock & Mari's was our favorite convenience store. It was run by a horse skeleton named Mari Lwyd and her husband, a straw-colored goat named Jul Bock.

I opened the door to their shop, and a little bell jingled.

"Ruprecht! Marley! Good tidings!" Bock greeted us as he pried himself away from a small television behind the counter. He wore a burlap robe and little red bows at the tip of each of his spiraling horns. From the sounds of it, he was watching a curling match.

As a fellow hooved Yuletopian, I felt an unspoken connection to Bock and Mari. They treated me like family, even though we barely knew each other at all. In the middle of a bustling, indifferent city, a friendly face can mean everything.

Mari emerged from one of the aisles holding a crate of sugar cookies. She and Bock walked on their hind legs, like me. "Hey, kids!" she said. She was draped in a white sheet and wore a thin crown of thorny holly on her skull. "Enjoying your winter break?"

"You could say that," said Marley. The moment we entered the store, she beelined to Bock and Mari's resident cat, Saturnalia. The poofy red cat rolled over on her back, purring loudly at Marley's approach.

"Heeey, Nalia," cooed Marley as she stroked the cat's impressive coat. "Such a pretty puffball."

"So far, winter break has been…memorable," I said. I plunged my claw into the large barrel of miniature candy canes they kept by the cash register. I dropped three heaping clawfuls onto the counter.

"HARK! This is a HARK News special bulletin!" A dramatic blare of trumpets interrupted the regular curling noises. We all turned our attention to the TV screen to see a suited otter holding a microphone, face twisted in worry.

The otter was standing in front of the jollification crime scene, which was still surrounded by red, white, and green tape. There was a TTPD car behind him with its lights off, and farther back loomed the dark trees of Belsnickel Park.

The otter cleared his throat and declared, "Late last night, there was what appears to be an intentional jollification on the banks of the Cinnamon River. The jollified elf, a tourist known as Sprinkles, is in stable condition. The perpetrator has not been apprehended, but our sources tell us a krampus is suspected. When reached for comment, Detective Metoh simply assured us that TTPD's finest were on the case."

The camera switched over to a squirrel with a swoopy hairdo. "A krampus jollifying an elf?" she asked, clicking her tongue and shaking her head. "And at this time of year? What is Tinseltown coming to?"

Bock clacked his hoof against the TV's Off button. The squirrel was gone, but my problems didn't leave with her.

Everyone was silent. Even Nalia stopped purring. I tossed a few chestnuts on the counter and loaded the candy canes into my pockets.

"Hey, Ruprecht," said Mari, her voice weighed down with worry. "You be careful out there, OK?"

I nodded to Mari, and then to Bock. "You too," I said. "Thanks for the canes."

As soon as the shop door closed behind us, Marley threw her hands in the air. "Why did they have to specify it was a krampus? Now every Townie on the street is going to eyeball you like you're a criminal."

"It's OK, Marley," I said as I readied a fresh candy cane. "I've had some time to get used to the feeling."

"Speaking of eyeballs, are we going to talk about that thing in the alley?" My gaze followed Marley's pointer finger to a pair of piercing green eyes peering out at us from a darkened alleyway across the street. They glowed like emeralds in the morning shadows.

"Maybe demons watch the news too," I said, trying to sound

tough, but feeling scared.

"It could be a demon or bad spirit that followed us from Specterville," said Marley as we hightailed it out of the creature's sightline. "Ignoring them is the best thing to do. It only makes it worse to pay attention to beings like that, or to show them fear. Let's stay alert and hope it minds its own business."

As we neared Polar Street, fluttering snowflakes thickened along with the morning crowds. It felt comforting to be surrounded by snowfall and so many Townies at once. It was easier to blend in, to feel unnoticed, unjudged, and blameless.

My head on a swivel, I stayed on high alert for those prowling green eyes. But we neared the ten-story hunk of ice known as the Ice Hotel and they did not make a return appearance.

The steady ringing of a bell guided us toward the entrance. It was in the hand of an elderly woman wearing a technicolor Christmas sweater. In front of her was a bucket, inside of which rested a meager smattering of chestnut bills. She had a cloud of thick white hair and wore a Christmas bulb earring in each ear. The earrings blinked in an alternating rhythm. By design, she was very difficult to ignore.

"Happy holidays, dears," she said, as if we were old friends. "If you can spare a chestnut for the Radiant Beams Orphanage, we'd be very grateful." Then she added with a loud chuckle, "And if not, no big whoop! Happy holidays all the same."

My hooves stopped involuntarily at the mention of Radiant Beams Orphanage. That was *my* orphanage. It's where my parents adopted me when I was a baby.

From my inside jacket pocket, I pulled out a big chunk of the chestnuts our client had paid us with. I handed it to the woman. "Happy holidays, ma'am," I said. "And a very happy new year."

Mouth open, the woman just blinked at me in rhythm with her earrings.

Marley and I snickered as we entered the ice-slab double doors of the Ice Hotel. They were big enough to let in a double-wide fleet of reindeer.

Behind us came a "Woo-hoo and hallelujah!" Apparently, the woman had snapped out of her initial shock. "It's a miracle on Polar Street!"

Marley went invisible as we entered the Ice Hotel's stately frozen lobby. I darted behind an imposing ice sculpture of a gingerbread family.

Quietly tapping my hoof, I waited until I heard gasping noises. Then I slipped through the lobby toward the elevators.

As I passed the front desk, I snuck a glance. Three posh-looking emperor penguin hotel employees were completely captivated by a poinsettia plant floating across the room.

With a smile, I pressed the 6 button in the ice elevator.

Marley appeared by my side as the ice cube hauled us up.

"That never gets old," she laughed. While not strictly necessary, distracting the front desk penguins allowed us to drop in on our client without giving him a warning. Plus, it was very fun.

We crept down a frigid corridor and stood in front of a door with an ornate number 651 etched into the ice. I rose a fist to knock, then glanced at Marley.

"Oh, right," she said, turning invisible. I nodded, and then I knocked.

The door opened a few inches with the chain lock in place. The elf appeared through the cracked door wearing the same green getup from Marley's house. He was standing on a stool, his flushed face eye level with me. He seemed even edgier than before, if that was possible.

"Did, uh, did you bring the cops?" he asked nervously.

"No, Mr. Rook," I said. "We kept our word."

"Did you tell the cops anything?" he asked.

"No, Mr. Rook," I said. "Pinky swear."

He closed the door, unlatched the chain lock, and fully opened it.

"I, uh, saw the news..." he said, hopping down from the stool.

I walked into the room and held the door open with my tail for a second so Marley could come in after me. I wasn't sure if she could teleport through solid ice.

We walked into a room of furry white furniture and I turned on the elf.

"Your story holds less water than a fishnet," I said, trying to use a calm voice. "What's really going on?"

"I'm so sorry about all of this!" the elf wailed. He ripped his hat off and balled it up in his little elf hands.

I plopped down on a fluffy sofa and propped my hooves on the plate-ice coffee table. I could feel Marley's presence somewhere to my right.

"I want to believe you, Mr. Rook," I said. "I really do."

The elf sighed. He seemed to be tearing up a little. Or at least trying to.

"That—that story I told you earlier was all—a story," he stammered. He looked at me with miserable frightened eyes.

Invisible Marley made a scoffing sound to my right. I coughed loudly to cover it up.

"Oh, that," I said lightly. I could hear soft rummaging noises in the hotel room. Marley was busy. "When we watched a krampus jollify an elf named Sprinkles, your story began to reek like expired eggnog."

The elf blushed and murmured, "I'm sorry I lied. I made up the story about a naughty brother, but the truth is, I'm the naughty one. I'm just a naughty elf who's lived a naughty life. But I swear—for once, I was trying to do the right thing."

"Listen, Mr. Rook," I said, and then stopped. A Yuletopia passport was floating toward me through the air. Marley materialized on the sofa and held it open.

The elf screamed and ducked beneath the coffee table. "Please, no ghosts!" he wailed.

The passport showed a picture of the elf, but his name wasn't Nowell Rook. It was Bajazzo.

"I'm sorry, Mr. Bajazzo," I said matter-of-factly. "When you lie to us, you lose your no-ghost privileges."

I crouched down and helped the elf up from under the table. "So, what else have you lied about? For example, did you have anything to do with that jollification?"

"No, no," said the elf. He was sitting across from us, wide eyes glued to Marley. "Please don't think that." Marley smiled back at him, pleasant as can be.

"Listen," I said, pointing at the snowflakes fluttering down on the other side of the icy window. "Out there is a yeti, an ice troll, and an entire city that knows a krampus jollified an elf in the middle of Tinseltown. And I'm the krampus they found at the crime scene."

I had the elf's attention. He blinked at me with a silly look on his face.

"Why did you send me to that bridge?"

The elf sighed. "It's about the snow globe. It's all about the snow globe."

"What about it?"

The elf stood up and approached a small pale turquoise Christmas tree in the corner of the room. He began to fidget with the blue icicle ornaments.

"That krampus and I were business partners, once," he said. The icicles clinked as he attempted to straighten them. His quaking hands only made it worse. "We met in Fangland, years ago. I had gained a reputation for acquiring precious objects in, let's say, less-than-legal ways. The krampus approached me to help him get the snow globe. I assumed he wanted it so he could sell it."

"And what makes it so special?" I asked. "What makes it different from any other snow globe?"

"The krampus would never tell," said the elf. "There's something about its origin that makes it not only very valuable, but apparently a powerful jollification weapon as well."

The elf continued to fiddle with the tree. He didn't seem like the type to be in cahoots with a loose-cannon krampus. But chestnuts had a funny effect on the brain.

"We had a deal," he continued. "He would pay me 50,000 chestnuts up front, and I would help him acquire the globe. Then we would go our separate ways. And that's what happened:

He paid me and I stole the globe. But then…"

The elf trailed off with his back to us. An icicle ornament dangled in his hand.

"But then I learned the krampus wasn't in this for the

money. I learned that his plan all along was to use the globe to jollify elves in Tinseltown. I couldn't let that happen. I had to do something, but I had a miles-long rap sheet that stopped me from going to the cops."

"You picked a nice sort of playmate," I said.

He turned around to face me. "So I sent you to the bridge, hoping you could intervene. I figured if anyone could stop a krampus, it would be another krampus."

"And what exactly was your plan?" Marley snapped. "You thought we'd show up to the bridge and do what? Fight the krampus?"

With a dramatic whirl away from the tree, the elf slumped back down in his chair.

"I don't know!" he wailed. "I'm good at stealing things, not at saving elves. It was a bad plan, but I had to try something. I thought maybe you could interrupt the jollification and help me track the krampus down. Or maybe you'd distract the krampus so the elf could escape."

"Didn't you think it might be a little dangerous to send Ruprecht into that situation?" asked Marley. "And that maybe he could be mistaken for the jollifier when the cops showed up?"

"I'm sorry!" said the elf. "I knew there would be an element of danger, but I thought that was part of the deal with private detectives. And it never occurred to me they'd mix up one krampus for another. I didn't mean to get you into hot water."

"OK, Mr. Bajazzo," I said, trying to maintain a professional tone. "So if the jollified elf isn't your brother, who is he?"

The elf shrugged. "Just some poor sap named Sprinkles from out of town. We're both from ponderosa trees, but I've never met him. I stole the photo from the krampus when I was spying on him."

"The Yule Kids and a goblin made a cameo appearance at the crime scene," said Marley. "Do you have any idea why?"

The elf shrugged again. "Word spreads fast in the Tinseltown crime world. I assume that every greedy villain in the city wants their hands on that globe. The Yule Kids are probably flying around trying to get it for their boss, Grýla. And I'd wager the goblin wants it too."

"Well, this all adds up to quite the Christmas carol," I said.

"I think it's time we sing it to the cops. Maybe they'll do a better job of avoiding another jollification."

The elf looked at me with frightened eyes.

"You won't…" he begged in a small, choked voice, "…go to the police?"

The elf stood up and reached a hand out to my forearm.

"I've done some naughty things to steal many valuable objects. If the cops find out I stole this globe as well, they'll toss me in the Cooler forever. Or worse—they'll send me to jail in Fangland."

I sighed. "Sorry, Mr. Rook…I mean, Mr. Bajazzo. Our detective/client relationship is over. We did what you paid us to do, now we have to protect the citizens of Tinseltown."

"Where are you going?" he asked.

"I'm going to do what I can to nab this jollifier, and that starts with telling the cops everything I know. I'll go to their station first thing tomorrow to spill my jelly beans. That leaves you some time to spill yours first. They'll be easier on you if you beat me to it, but that's up to you."

Marley whooshed past me and through the closed door. I opened the door and looked back at the elf. He was standing there in the center of the floor watching me leave with dazed brown eyes.

A small rattle of the poinsettia was all it took for Marley to give me cover to dart back through the lobby. Once outside, we worked our way through mobs of shopping Townies. The Radiant Beams lady had packed it up and left. Hopefully she was taking some well-earned time off.

"Our elf friend turned in quite a revision on his story," I said, a fresh candy cane rolling around in my mouth. "Do you buy it, Marley?"

"Not really," she said. "It's a little hard to trust the words of a professional thief, or at least someone who claims to be a professional thief."

"Agreed," I said. "Nice work rooting out the passport, by the way. Did you find anything else?"

"Unfortunately, no," she said. "The room was bare bones. In fact, it didn't seem like there was anyone staying there at all. There was no peppermint mouthwash, no night-light, no stuffed animals...there wasn't even eggnog in the fridge. There was nothing you'd expect to see in an elf's hotel room."

"So, he's likely staying somewhere else," I speculated. "Either he's from the area and using the Ice Hotel to throw someone off that scent, or he's crashing with a friend, or possibly at another hotel."

"That elf is fishier than a mermaid," said Marley. "We

should keep our eyes on him, but it's that jollifying krampus that poses the real threat."

"You're right," I said. "Even if the elf is a professional thief, he doesn't seem capable of causing real harm. But then again, appearances are about as useful as a Swiss cheese stocking."

We turned the corner onto Partridge Street. A newsy elf held a copy of the *Tinseltown Herald* high above his head. In a singsong rhythm, he hollered, "Hark! Intentional jollification in the midnight fog! No elf is safe! Hoofprints found on the scene! Cops suspect a krampus! A krampus jollifier is on the loose!"

Cringing at the mention of my species, I tried to sink my head into my shoulders. But it was a lost cause. Two suited business elves gawked in my direction, making a connection between the newsy elf's words and my face.

"Hey—what do you think you're looking at?" Marley zoomed over to them, her face supernaturally distorted with anger. "Staring is a good way to land on the naughty list."

The elves yelped and scampered off down the snowy sidewalk.

Their high-pitched squeals were interrupted by a clamor of terrified shrieks.

When I turned around, I saw that Marley was no longer scary looking—she was looking scared.

She pointed up above the rooftops on the other side of Partridge Street. It was those piercing green eyes again, but this time they were connected to a gigantic white cat. It was about the size of a one-horse open sleigh, horse included.

"That's one big kitty," said an awestruck Marley.

Its furry body blended in with the snow-covered rooftops. Its emerald eyes blazed through the white and stared down with an unnerving intensity.

The cat's eyes narrowed before it leaped elegantly from the rooftop onto the street.

Like an exploding zipper, the crowd frantically parted away from the cat. Their screams continued as they cleared a path directly in front of us.

With nothing between us, the green-eyed cat crouched down like a stalking tiger, only a whole lot bigger.

My heart was beating as fast as a mouse's. But this cat looked like it was craving something much bigger than a mouse. Something roughly the size of a twelve-year-old krampus.

Paying no mind to the panicking elves, the cat zeroed in on its prey. Slinking silently toward me, green eyes locked on its petrified target, the giant cat took up most of the street and all of my wits.

"You'd better get out of here, Ruprecht," Marley whispered. And she wasn't kidding.

The cat was closing in. Its pupils constricted into vertical slits and its back hair hardened into jagged spikes. When its tail twitched and its butt wiggled, I knew it was time to move it or lose it.

I burst down a nearby alley and inside the closest shelter I could find: the back door of a gift-wrapping store called All Wrapped Up in Christmas. I didn't care where I was, as long as that cat wasn't using my bones as toothpicks.

When we got inside the gift-wrapping store, my breath caught in my throat and I froze like a snow cone.

"Ruprecht...?" Marley was just as astonished.

It wasn't a gift-wrapping store at all. Not even a little bit.

Marley and I were in a lush and beautiful forest overflowing with lichen, moss, mushrooms, and evergreens. A thin layer of snow dusted the forest floor.

After a second of confusion, I exhaled with relief and muttered, "Witchcraft."

"Duh," said Marley, pretending to slap her forehead. "Of course."

Down a crude stone path, I walked and Marley floated toward a little brick cottage with grass growing on the roof. The door opened right in time with our approach to reveal a beautiful witch.

She wore a resplendent red-velvet hooded cape, black

boots, and a warm smile. She had wavy white hair and held a tall, knotty wooden staff. At the top of the staff rested a glowing green orb with brilliant curtains of greens and blues and purples swirling inside.

"Hello, Ruprecht," said the witch.

I said, "Hey, Mom," and gave her a hug.

CHAPTER SIX

FRAU PERCHTA

"I'm sorry if Jóla scared you, dear," said my mom. She was stirring a cast-iron pot on the stove. Marley and I were seated at a little wooden table.

"That cat is a friend of yours?" I breathed a sigh of relief knowing that white fluffy terror wasn't trying to eat me. She was trying to corral me. "There are less terrifying ways to get my attention, you know."

"Unfortunately, I can't just swoop down on you in a crowd of holiday shoppers to get your attention," said my mom. "I still feel guilty about accidentally jollifying that elf last winter. I have to be careful about my public appearances, especially in Tinseltown."

My mom, Frau Perchta, is a beloved icon of holiday magic and one of Yuletopia's biggest celebrities. Many elves, especially Townies not used to spending time with her, can't handle the rush of holiday spirit that her presence inspires.

"And don't worry, sugarplum," she said, as she reached into a small cupboard. "Jóla wouldn't harm you. She's a kind and noble creature. I met her while chasing the wicked ogre Leppalúdi through some lava fields. She helped me capture him. We hit it off right away."

My mom set a cup of cocoa down in front of me and sat at the table. She leaned her staff against the wall beside her, its green sphere swirling sleepily. She never let her staff outside of arm's reach. Especially this close to the solstice.

I took a sip of the cocoa and marveled at its realistic taste. Although I knew all of this was just a figment of my mom's magic, it all felt so very real: the smell and sound of crackling cedar in the fireplace, the detailed brick and mortar of the cabin walls, the crows cawing outside, and the winter sun streaking through the window against my face.

I tried to enjoy the moment, but I knew this conversation wasn't going to be all about cocoa and sunshine.

My mom rested her chin on her hand and ever so slightly raised an eyebrow. I took another sip of cocoa and braced myself.

"I received an alarming call from Detective Metoh," she said. "He told me that you and Marley were at the scene of a jollification. That's why I asked Jóla to shadow you and make sure you were safe."

She placed her hand on my forearm. "I know your dad and I promised to give you your space over winter break, but this changes things considerably."

"Yeah, I could see that," I said, returning her gaze.

She leaned back in her chair. "Metoh also tells me you two started your own detective agency."

I set my cocoa on the table and interlaced my claws. With a small smile, I gave her my best impression of a calm and collected krampus. She wasn't buying it.

"I admire the initiative, Ruprecht. And you too, Marley. But maybe, given recent events, we should put the detective business on hold?"

When I didn't respond, she returned her hand to my arm.

"As you know, there is a slender veil that separates our world from others. And, as you know, that veil grows thinner as we approach the darkest day of the year, the Winter Solstice. This time of year, I have my hands completely tied protecting the realm from evil-hearted and otherworldly creatures who want nothing more than to run amok in Yuletopia. It's never a good idea to mess around with dark forces, and that's doubly true in December."

"I know, Mom," I said, trying to sound like one adult talking to another. "I'm trying to help too, in my own way. There's a krampus out there jollifying elves, and the cops don't seem to have a suspect besides me. I can't just walk away from that."

"I appreciate that you want to help, Ruprecht, but you're only twelve."

"Don't fret, Frau P, I'll take care of him," Marley chimed in. She was doing her valiant best to lighten the tone. "Technically I've been around for 188 years, so I have enough experience for the both of us."

My mom responded with a warm smile. "And speaking of experience, what do you two know about this jollification?" she asked. "Metoh thinks you might have information you're not sharing."

Bluffing the cops was one thing. But there was no way I was going to pull anything over on my mom.

So, I took a deep breath and told her everything. I told her about Bajazzo (a.k.a. Nowell Rook), Bajazzo's fake story, Bajazzo's revised story, the jollification, the limping krampus, the snow globe, the cops, the Yule Kids, the goblin. All of it.

As I told my story, my mom's worried look worsened. At the mention of the Yule Kids, she reached reflexively for her staff. She was now rolling it lightly in her slender fingers.

"If that snow globe is as valuable as that elf says," she thought out loud, "Grýla will have her greedy eyes all over it. And while that explains the Yule Kids, the jollification doesn't sit right. No krampus I've met would ever jollify an elf. Long ago, krampuses used fear as a motivator, but this krampus is doing something very different. He's using joy as a weapon."

"The way he laughed, Mom," I said with a cringe. "It didn't sound right. It sounded deranged."

My mom gave me a frown. "It's a naughty world out there," she said. "You're a smart kid, but you're too young to be taking it all head on."

"It's possible I bit off a little more gingerbread than I can chew," I said with a sigh. "I really wanted to be the hero so that I'd stop getting blamed for things. So that everyone would stop looking at me with suspicion."

She put her hand on my shoulder. "So you'll tell the cops what you've told me?"

"Yes," I said. "The best I can do now is let the cops do their thing, even if it doesn't result in the city honoring me with a ticker tape parade down Santa Claus Lane."

"Good," said my mom. "And I know you may not like it,

but I'm going to ask Jóla to continue shadowing you until this jollification business is solved."

Most of the private detectives I've read about don't have giant feline bodyguards. But I knew there was no point in arguing.

My mom gathered us together in the middle of the cottage. She raised her staff above our heads.

"Be careful, you two," she said. She muttered an incantation under her breath. "*Magia silva evanescet…tabernam reditus normalis…*"

In a snap, the forest cottage was replaced by the gift-wrapping store on Partridge Street.

An elf shrieked. She was holding a tape gun and wearing a wrapping-paper uniform with a bow on her head. Her mouth was wide open as she stared at the krampus and the ghost who had materialized out of nowhere in the middle of her store.

Slowly, the tape gun slid out of her hand and clattered onto the floor.

"Season's greetings," I said with a nod.

"Happy holidays," said Marley with a small bow.

The elf kept staring. I cleared my throat, and we left.

It was midafternoon when we got back to Marley's. We had taken the Avalanche Express bus line and watched as Jóla nimbly trailed us, skillfully slinking atop fire escape ledges and snowy rooftops.

When Marley and I got inside, the giant cat found a large gabled roof across the street to curl up around and wait. She seemed very committed to her bodyguard role.

While I dashed to the pantry for a snack, Marley floated to the parlor to check her dad's spirit box for messages. It was the ghost world's version of voice mail.

From the kitchen, I could hear the recording of a gruff voice fill the parlor. "Ruprecht, it's Metoh," said the voice. "You need to call us ASAP."

After a beep, a higher-pitched voice followed. It was my oldest brother. "Hey, Ruprecht, and hey, Marley. It's Otto. I heard the news and wanted to check in. Mom and Dad seem worried. Call me when you can."

I joined Marley in the parlor with a plate of cold mince-meat pies, but before I had a chance to take a bite, Marley's old-fashioned wall phone jangled with urgency.

Marley shrugged at me and I shrugged back. We both knew we should answer it. I set my pies down on a side table and walked to the phone. Marley floated over to listen in.

Pulling the receiver to my ear, I played the part of a cheery office assistant. "Krampus and Marley, confidential investigations. How may I direct your call?"

"Cut the cute stuff," hissed Schnee's ice-cold voice. "Where've you been? There's been another jollification, and conveniently, you've been missing all morning."

My heart sank at the news. Bajazzo was right—this krampus was hooked on jollifying.

"I'm very sorry to hear that, Sergeant," I said. "But I've been with my mom and Marley. You can ask them. Who was the victim?"

She ignored my question. "Have you been in the Pagan Hill neighborhood at any point today?"

I looked at Marley, and she nodded. Lying would make a bad thing worse. "Yes," I said. "I was there this morning. I get my candy canes at Bock & Mari's. They'll tell you the same."

"Imagine that," said Schnee with mock wonder. "Another incredible coincidence. Once again, we find you in the vicinity of a jollification."

I heard a muffled exchange before Metoh's voice filled the receiver. "Listen, Ruprecht," he said. "You need to tell us everything you know. Otherwise, you're still a suspect. And the jollifications are piling up."

"Funny you should say that, Detective," I said, adding a chipper shine to my delivery. "I was just about to suggest the same thing. How about first thing tomorrow?"

"Oh, well, great," said the yeti. He was doing a bad job of hiding his surprise. "We'll be up to our ears in paperwork the rest of the day, anyway. We'll see you at the Halls of Justice at, say, 8 a.m."

Then, after an awkward pause, he cleared his throat and added, "That's a good krampus. I, uh, knew you'd come around."

I hung up the phone and turned to Marley. "Well, it's official. We're dealing with a serial jollifier."

This terrible news, and those terrible words—serial jollifier—draped over the rest of our afternoon like a grim shroud.

Marley headed to her organ room to give the feeling a soundtrack. I stayed in the parlor to call my brother back, hoping it would take my mind off things.

When I was done talking to Otto, he passed the phone to the next sibling, and so on down the line. It took 90 minutes to chat with all six of them. In addition to Otto, there was Annike, Brunhilda, Elias, Elke, and Fritz. It was all very pleasant, but phone calls can be a bit of a time suck when you have a family as big as mine.

One by one, I assured them all that I was doing fine and perfectly safe. I told them if they didn't believe me, they could talk to the colossal cat parked out front.

I hadn't slept right in days, and though the sky was barely beginning to darken, I desperately needed some shut-eye. Or at least I needed to give it a shot.

Before heading upstairs, I peeked out the front window and saw that Jóla didn't share my sleeping problem. She was out there catnapping peacefully right where we'd left her, a thin layer of snow accumulating on her fur.

Then I poked my head into Marley's organ room beside the parlor. We agreed to get in some early morning research before our appointment with the cops.

We exchanged our "goodnights" and I lit a candle. As I creaked my way up the wooden stairs, Marley's melancholy music echoed through the walls once again.

At the top of the stairs, I opened the door to my room, closed it, and turned to the bed.

"Aah!" I cried, jumping back and nearly dropping the candle.

There, sitting on the end of my bed, was a green-skinned goblin staring at me with a wicked smile stretched across his face. He was roughly the size and shape of a holiday ham.

He sat with long, thin legs crossed, the willowy fingers of

one hand holding a small silver double-bit ax. He tapped the ax threateningly against the palm of his other hand. He wore a red plaid cloak with white shoes that curled at his toes into long points. On his head perched a broad-brimmed hat decorated with a single turkey feather.

I had seen this goblin before. He was the one who'd bounced out of the trees to make way for the cackling krampus.

"Please, Mr. Krampus," said the goblin. "Have a seat." His pleasant tone was somewhat counteracted by dozens of sharp dark-yellow teeth. Not to mention the ax.

The goblin gestured toward the chair beside my bed. I kept my eyes on the ax and did what he said. It was enchanted, by the looks of it. More suited to disintegrating molecules than chopping wood.

"I apologize for the impolite entrance," said the goblin. "There's a very large feline watching the front door from a nearby rooftop, so I had to crawl in through your bedroom window. I do hope you understand."

My heart was racing, but I had to play it cool. I gave the goblin a small shrug.

"I'll just get down to it," said the goblin. "My name is Pickwick, and I'm trying to recover an—ah—ornament that has been—shall we say—mislaid? I thought, and hoped, you could assist me."

The goblin spoke slowly, carefully selecting each word. "The ornament isn't for a tree, it's for a mantel," he said. "It's a snow globe. It's normal-looking for a snow globe: it has a house, some trees, snow swirling around."

I nodded with big eyes to indicate attentiveness.

"And I know you have it. But I'm not here to rob you, I'm here to buy it from you."

"If you're here to buy it, then what's with the ax?"

"You're a krampus," said the goblin without emotion. "And I saw you jollify an elf and disappear in a cloud of smoke. Who knows what else you're capable of?"

"You've got the wrong krampus," I said. "It was a foggy night, sure, but you're confusing me with someone taller, older, and a lot more evil."

"I have reason to believe I'm not mistaken," said the goblin confidently. "And I'm prepared to pay the sum of 5,000 chestnuts for the snow globe's recovery." The goblin touched a cloth sack slung around his side.

"Five thousand is a lot of chestnuts," I said, looking thoughtfully at the goblin. "But that wasn't my snow globe, and I'm not that krampus."

"Suit yourself," he said, hopping down from the bed. Despite his long legs, he was still much shorter than me. "Then I'm forced to search for it. Oh, and I should mention that one swing in your direction with this ax and you will explode like a party popper. So, please, clasp your claws behind your head and sit tight while I search your room for the globe."

"Go ahead and search," I said. I tried to calm my pulse. Outwardly, my expression was neutral, but inside, my mind was twisting itself into knots trying to think of a way out of this jam.

The goblin took two steps toward the bookshelf and stopped.

He grunted with confusion, and then squealed. He grabbed his nose as if he'd been pinched, and his ax swung out of his hand and across the room.

As I caught the ax, Marley appeared beside the goblin. She was holding his sack.

"Nice move, Marley," I said, testing the weight of the ax.

"Nice catch," she said.

The goblin's face was twisted with fear and disappointment. There were tears forming in his eyes.

I took a step toward him and pointed the ax at the bed. "Please, Pickwick," I said politely. "Have a seat."

I held the ax and kept an eye on the goblin as Marley removed the contents from the bag, one item at a time, and arranged everything neatly on the floor.

There was a worn-out Yuletopia passport with Pickwick's name and portrait. In the last year alone, he'd had his passport stamped far and wide in places like Franke, Morassia, Deadmark, and Reptilia.

There was a snapshot of a young goblin in a church's graveyard with a mischievous grin.

There was a large turkey feather (apparently in case he lost the one in his hat).

There was a notecard with Marley's address written in small, neat letters: 33 Hereafter Avenue.

And, finally, there was a chestnut-stuffed envelope. Marley counted the money and announced there were only 800 chestnuts total—not the 5,000 promised by the goblin.

"Five thousand chestnuts, Pickwick?" I asked with a raised eyebrow.

"I wasn't lying," he said. "I don't have that much on me, but I can—and will—get it if the globe turns up."

Then after a pause, he asked, "You have it?"

"No," I said. "Still don't have it. But you have certainly piqued my curiosity. Why is everyone climbing over each other to get at this snow globe? What about it makes it such a powerful jollification weapon?"

"Surely you must know as much as I do." The goblin seemed genuinely confused.

"Just assume that I know nothing," I said. "Now, please, lay your cards on the table."

"All I know," said the goblin, "is that the criminals of Tinseltown can't stop talking about the extraordinary value of this snow globe. I figured if anyone had a bead on it, it would be Grýla. The Yule Kids work for Grýla, so I tailed them for a few days. One foggy night, they led me to the edge of Belsnickel Park near the Glacé Bridge. It was there that I saw you use the snow globe to jollify an elf. To make the jollification happen, you recited the globe's origin story, and the elf couldn't help himself. The story was far too much for him to handle."

"Oh, yeah?" I said. "And what story was that?"

"That snow globe is Santa's first toy," he said.

Marley and I exchanged a look. The goblin continued. "Inside the globe is a model of the wooden shed that served as Santa's first workshop in the Laughing Valley. This was the first Christmas gift he ever made."

I narrowed my eyes. "What else do you know, Pickwick?"

The goblin leaned forward. "I also happen to know that you were raised by the fat man in the North Pole. Santa Claus is your father."

CHAPTER SEVEN

THE TINSELTOWN HALLS OF JUSTICE

The goblin was right. My full name is Ruprecht Claus-Perchta. My parents, Santa Claus and Frau Perchta, adopted me from Radiant Beams Orphanage in Tinseltown when I was a baby. I grew up in the Christmas Castle in the North Pole.

The last name brings attention, so I don't use it when I don't have to. In Yuletopia, the "Perchta" half is just as attention-grabbing as the "Claus" side. Putting them together creates a powder keg of unwanted publicity.

"And what's that to you?" I asked the goblin calmly.

"It's nothing to me, Mr. Krampus," he said. "I'm not casting judgment. I figured you were behind the jollifications because you have access to the inner chambers of the Christmas Castle, where I presume the snow globe comes from. Plus," he gestured in my direction, "you are a krampus and I saw you do it."

"Well, I hate to spoil your holiday wishes, but I'm not the krampus you're looking for," I said.

"Again, no judgment," said the goblin. "I don't care what you've done or why you did it—I just want the globe."

"Again, I'm sorry to disappoint," I said. I handed the goblin his sack. Marley had repacked it. "Here's your stuff. And you can keep your chestnuts. Apparently, Marley and I are the only souls in Tinseltown not addicted to the stuff."

"Suit yourself, Mr. Krampus," said the goblin. "If you change your mind, here's my card."

He placed a card on my desk and then hesitated. "May I have my ax?"

"Sure," I said. I handed him the small silver ax, and he quickly pointed it at my chest.

"Please keep your claws where I can see them," he said earnestly. "I intend to search this place for the snow globe. And no funny business, ghost."

Marley rolled her eyes, and I laughed for the first time in a while. "All right, Pickwick," I said. "We won't stop you."

After the goblin left, disappointed and empty-handed, I spent the night barely sleeping. Visions of two-faced elves, swarming Yule Kids, and cackling krampuses danced in my head.

It was still dark when I crawled out of bed. In a groggy haze, I shuffled down the hall to Marley's study.

The door was open. She was on the floor surrounded by teetering stacks of books. She had a head start on the research,  and by the looks of it, that head start had begun many hours ago.

When I knocked on the doorframe, a wild-eyed Marley popped her head up from a hulking tome. She looked something like a possessed college student.

"Ruprecht!" she yelled. "I've looked through the last 300 years of Tinseltown crime records—there's not a single report of a krampus jollifier." She laughed with abandon. "Can you believe it? Not one! And this krampus has done it twice."

She pointed to a thermos and a mug shaped like a moose's head with antlers for handles. "Oh, and I made some cider."

"Thanks, Marley," I said, sliding into the desk chair and pulling the thermos toward me. "So this krampus jollifier is one of a kind. Like some kind of wicked snowflake."

"Exactly," she said. "And by the way, I can't find any historical record of your dad making a snow globe in the Laughing Valley."

"That's the thing, Marley," I said, filling the mug with piping-hot cider. "I've always been told my dad's first toy was a wooden cat. I think someone's pulling someone's chain about the snow globe's origin."

"And yet, it still does the trick as a jollification weapon," she said.

"I guess stories don't have to be true to have power," I said. "Like how half of the North Pole thinks I released that poltergeist. The fakeness of the story didn't stop me from getting suspended."

Marley returned to her books and I blew on the steaming moose mug. I took a sip, looked into the mug, and sprayed cider all over the desk.

A face was beaming back at me from inside, and it wasn't mine.

"Hey, kids!" said the face.

"Hi, Mr. Marley," I said, recovering from the shock. Marley's dad wore spectacles and a ponytail-type hairstyle that must have been popular when he was alive.

"Dad!" said Marley. "You're going to scare him stiff. Please, just materialize normally."

The face disappeared from my mug and a full-bodied ghost in his early fifties appeared beside the desk. As always, he was draped in chains, padlocks, and cashboxes. He was gray and shimmery, just like his daughter.

"Sorry, love," he said with a chuckle. He pulled a ghostly handkerchief from his pocket and dabbed up my cider spray. "It's an old habit I have to kick."

Mr. Marley surveyed the mounds of books covering the floor. "Are you early birds getting in some predawn research?"

"Yep, you know us!" said Marley with a slight strain in her voice. "Just a couple of bookworms."

"Very good," said Mr. Marley. "I'm just stopping in for a jiff before my next appointment. How's your winter break coming along? Up to anything interesting?"

Even before Mr. Marley could finish the final syllable on the word "interesting," Marley piped in, a bit too loudly. "We're fine! Everything is fine! It's good to see you, Dad. Happy Christmas and all that."

"Well, it's good to see you too, Viv," said Mr. Marley, slightly taken aback. He cleared his throat and turned to me, causing his chains to jangle.

"Ruprecht, the Ghost of Christmas Present has spirited in some cured salmon. I thought you might like some."

"Thanks, Mr. Marley, that sounds delicious," I said, and I wasn't lying.

After giving his daughter a peck on the head, Mr. Marley whisked out of sight in a spirally flourish of mist.

We headed down to the kitchen. "I'm so glad he doesn't follow current events," said Marley. "I don't think he's read a newspaper in a hundred years."

I gulped down a plate of cured salmon with an apple cider chaser. The salmon, fished from the Cinnamon River, had a strong cinnamony aftertaste. It was just OK, but it delivered some much-needed energy into my system.

It was almost time to head to the station to give the cops the full spiel. But it would make for a much better story if the central character, Bajazzo, was there to help me tell it.

Marley used her wall phone to call the front-desk penguins at the Ice Hotel. She adopted a posh, aristocratic accent that I found hilarious.

"Why, hello!" she blared, adding ornate flourishes to every syllable. "I'm phoning to speak to my great-grandnephew, a little elf in room 651."

I could hear a penguin squawking on the other end of the line. If only these tuxedo birds knew they were again being duped by a ghost.

"Ah, he checked out late last night, you say?" Marley repeated the penguin's words so I could follow along. "Quite interesting. I must say, good sir, I find myself in quite the pickle. I have a plate of Christmas cookies to deliver to my grandnephew, uh, great-grandnephew, but I'm not sure how to reach him. Did he happen to mention where he was going?"

Marley listened to the squawking and nodded along.

"Ah, he didn't mention where he was going." She considered the situation, and then her bright white eyes lit up with a thought. "Thank you, sir. I do have one more small and unrelated question to ask: When does room service turn the sheets? At eleven? OK, thank you. Why, you ask? Oh, no reason. I have become quite nosy in my old age. I'm afraid I can't help it."

Marley hung up the phone, and I applauded her quick thinking. The elf may never talk to the cops, but he might have left some clues behind that could do all the talking for him. There was only one way to find out, but we had to get moving.

I slugged back the rest of my cider, I stuck a fresh candy cane in my cheek, and we were off.

From the front window, I could see the big cat curled

around a snowcapped chimney across the street. Her giant satellite-dish ears perked up immediately when the door opened. I gave her a sarcastic salute.

It felt a tad belittling to have a monster-cat babysitter, but if I was honest, it was a little comforting too.

I bit down on my candy cane, crammed my claws into my pockets, and leaned in against the wind.

It was December 19. With the big day looming, Tinseltown was in its full holiday buzz, despite the early hour. Jóla shadowed from above as we passed clusters of early morning shoppers, joyriding sleighs, and shiny decorations plastered onto every lamppost, windowsill, and doorway.

It was all pleasant in its way, a communal brightness and warmth in the midst of moaning wind and icy flurries. It would have been nice to soak it in, but this stuff was for people with time on their hands. And time was the last thing you'd find stuffed inside my toy sack.

When we reached the Ice Hotel, I saddled up near a quartet of caroling gumdrop elves. One of them used an accordion to guide the others toward a consistent tempo, but it was a lost cause. They certainly gave it their all.

Marley blinked out of visibility and floated into the hotel and up to the sixth floor to look for clues. She went alone because she could work more quickly that way, and because Jóla wouldn't be happy if I left her sight.

The big cat was sitting on top of a parked milk truck, her head cocked uncertainly in my direction. I gave her a shrug, and she just kept staring.

After a few minutes, I heard a disembodied whisper in my ear as a paper-wrapped item slipped into my claw. "OK, Rupe," said the voice. "Let's get out of here."

"Well? Is this some sort of clue?" I asked as I rejoined the crowd. A few heads in front of me turned around to shoot concerned looks at the excited krampus walking around and talking to himself.

"No," said Marley, blipping into visibility. "Say what you will about that elf, but he is spick-and-span. All I found were mint candy wrappers and this fruitcake."

I looked at the paper-wrapped loaf in my claw.

"So why'd you nab the fruitcake?" I asked.

"Who knows how long they'll keep us at the station," she said. "You might get hungry. And you living folks don't think straight when you're hungry."

"Thanks, Marley," I said, and I stashed the fruitcake in my pocket.

Marley floated next to me as I hoofed up the slick stone steps of the Tinseltown Halls of Justice. The Tinseltown Police Station and Courthouse were located within, and beneath both of them was the Tinseltown Jailhouse, otherwise known as the Cooler.

Stately structural columns lined the front of the building. On either side stood two giant expressionless stone reindeer statues. These weren't the kind that stood on their hind hooves like me. These were the intimidating all-fours kind of reindeer, like those in my dad's fleet.

With Jóla lying across several rows of steps behind us, Marley and I neared the entrance. On the way, we passed a copper statue of a snowman wearing a blindfold. Stick hands outstretched, the snowman balanced a handful of chestnuts in one hand, a handful of coal in the other.

Reaching for the large glass door, I jumped back as my entire frame of vision suddenly brimmed with blindingly white polar bear fur.

"Mr. Claus-Perchta," said a polar bear guard in a voice deeper than the Crystalline Sea. He was holding out a table-size paw to stop us. "We've been expecting you."

He looked at Marley with a dash of judgment. "She can join you, but only sheeted ghosts can enter the courthouse."

"Forget it," Marley said, crossing her arms irritably. "There's no way."

To restrict a ghost's ability to go invisible, escape, cause mischief, or otherwise sneak around, Tinseltown government buildings require that all ghosts wear a white sheet with eyeholes cut out. Of course, any self-respecting ghost found the rule completely demeaning.

"It's OK, Marley," I said. "I'm sure this will be quick. We can spare you the indignity."

"Good luck, Ruprecht," she said. "Remember—the truth is on your side."

The unchatty bear escorted me inside the building and down an unfriendly hallway.

I unwrapped a candy cane and walked to the other side of the hall to toss the wrapper into a copper bin. The polar bear whipped around.

"Hey! Where are you going?" he barked. He used paws I couldn't argue with to corral me in front of him. "How about you walk where I can see you."

I held up my claws to show I meant no offense. "I'm just trying not to litter, pal."

We wound our way past Townies in various states of

emotional stress. Some sobbed, some argued, and others muttered angrily to nobody in particular.

Unless you worked here, the Halls of Justice didn't seem like a place you wanted to be. Especially this time of year.

We approached a front desk with a tired-looking iguana on the phone behind it. He was wearing a gaudy Christmas sweater with a knitted image of my dad riding a T. rex. The jolly nature of his sweater stood in stark contrast with his mood.

The iguana eyed us with a distinct lack of interest and said into the phone receiver, "I understand, ma'am. The gremlin is stuck in your chimney. OK, yes. That must be very stressful. I understand. Ma'am? I'm going to have to put you on hold for a moment. Just one moment. OK, thank you."

The iguana sighed, closed his eyes, and seemed to collect himself.

"The krampus kid is here," said the polar bear.

"Yes, thank you, Bob," said the iguana, opening his eyes. "I can very much see that. I'll take it from here."

The polar bear grunted and headed back down the hall. Small tremors quivered through the floor with each thunderous step.

"How do you do, Mr. Claus-Perchta?" asked the iguana. He stood up and walked around the desk. "Metoh and Schnee are eager to speak with you, as I'm sure you're aware."

"Yeah," I said. "I was beginning to suspect that was the case."

"Well aren't you the little detective?" he said with a wink.

I followed him into a dingy, empty office room. There was a table, a coffee maker with hot coffee, and a tray of stale-looking saffron buns beside it.

The iguana held a scaly hand toward one of the chairs. "Coffee? Bun?" he asked.

"No thanks," I said, pointing to my mouth as I sat down. "It might spoil my candy cane."

"Suit yourself," he said, as if he meant it. "They'll be in here soon. Just relax."

"Soon" was an understatement. I barely had the chance to draw a breath before Schnee marched in like a blizzard with Metoh lumbering in behind her.

Behind Metoh came an old timid-looking elf no taller than the table. The elf had a long white beard, wore a visor, and held a notebook.

Metoh and Schnee sat across from me. The elf hopped up on a stool and uncapped a pen.

Schnee glared her usual glare while Metoh leaned back

to get a better look at me, like a therapist analyzing their client.

"I know you won't mind if this is on the record, will you, Ruprecht?" Schnee hadn't blinked since her eyes first locked onto me.

I chuckled. "As long as you don't forget to say that everything I say can be used against me."

"Good," said Schnee. "So who's been jollifying elves?"

"I don't know," I said. The elf scribbled on his pad. "How are the elves, by the way? I assume that, like Sprinkles, the newest elf was also a tourist taking in the holiday sights?"

Metoh and Schnee shared a look, and they didn't try to hide it.

Metoh leaned to his right and rested his chin in his paw. "The elves are expected to fully recover, but someone has put them through some trauma. And perhaps you don't know who that someone is, but I bet you could make an excellent guess."

I rolled the candy cane in my mouth a bit before answering. "Maybe," I said. "But I wouldn't."

Metoh and Schnee were taken aback. The elf stopped scribbling and looked at me, eyes wide.

"Because guessing would be silly," I said, cool as an icicle. "I might have a good guess, or I might have a bad one. But my parents didn't raise me to make wild guesses about jollifications in front of two cops and a stenographer."

"Now, Ruprecht. Guessing isn't so bad if you have nothing to hide." Metoh's tone was neutral. Inviting, even.

"We all have something to hide," I said. "Especially around Christmastime."

"I know you're having fun playing detective," said Schnee, "but this tough guy talk isn't going to help." Somehow, her patience felt even more nonexistent than before.

Metoh rubbed the bridge of his blue nose with his fingers. The elf seemed to note that in his book.

Schnee got up from the table and poured herself a cup of coffee. Hoarfrost coated the outside of the mug as she held it with both hands. In just a few seconds, she had turned hot coffee into a coffee slushy. It was very impressive, I had to admit.

"Schnee may disagree with me," said Metoh, "but I don't think you meant to do anything bad. I think you got involved in something without knowing what it was—"

"I see," I said. "You don't think I'm naughty. You think I'm clueless."

"No, Ruprecht, far from it," said Metoh. "I think you're too smart to think it would be a good idea to withhold information from the cops."

I sighed and placed my claws on the arms of my chair. "You're exactly right, Metoh," I said. "I'm here to tell you every-thing. At first I thought I was doing the right thing by protecting my client. But that ship has sailed. It's too dangerous."

Schnee slammed her coffee slushy on the table, causing it to slosh around in the mug. "You're twelve!" she cried. "Twelve-year-olds don't have clients!"

Metoh put a big paw on her shoulder. "Come on, Schnee. Let's hear what the kid has to say."

Schnee shook her head and took a sip of her slushy to compose herself.

I nodded to the stenographer elf. He nodded back and cracked his knuckles, and I started yapping.

Beginning with the tree elf shaking in Marley's parlor, I told them everything I had told my mom, with the addition of Pickwick's visit and his snow globe origin story. The cops listened intently as the stenographer feverishly filled the pages of his notebook.

When I finished, I took a deep breath and slumped down in my chair.

"Thank you, Ruprecht," said Metoh. "You've done a great service to Tinseltown. Your mom and dad would be proud."

"So that's the nonfiction version of events," I said. "Have you heard from this Bajazzo character for his version?"

"Usually we wouldn't share that kind of information with a civilian," said Metoh. "But since you've been so cooperative, the answer is no. We haven't heard from an elf named Bajazzo…

or Nowell Rook, for that matter."

The yeti pulled out a walkie-talkie. The ice troll scowled, as if my story wasn't digesting well.

Glancing at his notes, the yeti squeezed the walkie-talkie and growled: "Put out an all-points bulletin for a ponderosa tree elf, three feet tall, flaxen hair, acorn backpack. Yuletopia passport under name 'Bajazzo.' 'Nowell Rook' is a known alias. Do the same for a goblin named Pickwick—also three feet tall, wide-brimmed hat, turkey feather. Weapons include a silver ax. Also has a Yuletopia passport."

Schnee's eyes tightened as she continued to stare. "I don't know, Metoh. We gave this kid a couple days to come up with a wild story filled with nonsense. It all smells like make believe to me, including the all-too-perfect detail that the snow globe is his dad's first toy."

"I already told you that I think the goblin's story is bogus," I said. "On at least that point, we're in agreement."

Schnee turned to her partner as if I wasn't in the room. "We know he has a history of elaborate pranks," she said. "This could just be his and the ghost's latest grasp for attention."

The yeti grunted. "It is quite the story," he said, "so we're going to fact-check every last word. And Ruprecht's too smart to leave town or go anywhere we can't find him. Isn't that right, Ruprecht?"

"That's right, Metoh," I said. "I'm not hard to miss—just look for the giant cat tailing me everywhere I go." Then, with my claws on the chair's armrests, I blurted, "OK if I clear out?"

"Yes, you can go," grunted Metoh. With a playful smirk, he added, "But remember—your dad isn't the only one who sees you when you're sleeping and knows when you're awake."

Then Schnee snapped in a far less playful manner: "So you better watch out!"

"Don't worry, I'll be good," I said as I walked out of the room. "If only for goodness' sake."

CHAPTER EIGHT

THE FIRST TOY

Billowing clouds smudged out the sky. It was late morning when I left the Halls of Justice, but as far as lighting went, it might as well have been dusk.

The giant cat was lying down where we'd left her on the building's grand steps. The winter winds gently whisked her long white fur.

When the glass doors clicked shut behind me, the cat's whiskers twitched, her emerald eyes popped open, and her ears shifted toward me like the sails of a schooner. When she stood up, several passerby elves jumped and darted out of her pouncing range.

Marley burst in beside me before my hoof hit the first step.

"So, how'd it go? Did they put you through the wringer?"

"No, not really," I said, walking slowly down the steps. "They're good cops, when it comes down to it. But their bedside manner leaves some room for improvement."

When we reached the bottom step, I took a deep breath and sat down. A gush of exhaustion rolled over me like a crashing wave. On the steps behind us, Jóla sat grooming herself, patiently waiting for our next move.

"It felt good to get it all out there in the open," I said. "Now the cops are on the hunt for our former client, so we just have to sit back and see how the gumdrops fall."

"I really hope they track him down," said Marley. "Something tells me that if they can find him, they can find the jollifying krampus."

"Yeah," I said. "It could be the elf is trying to scurry away because he feels scared, or it could be that he feels guilty. And it's possible that it's both."

We sat on the steps, lost in silent thought. My tiredness made everything feel thin and intangible, like a dream under construction. That interview had taken a lot out of me, and it seemed like years since I'd slept well.

"What do you say we hail a sleigh, Marley? I'm beat."

"Of course, Ruprecht," she said. "But we'll have to cross the street to catch one heading in the right direction."

We stood up, and I walked and she floated to the crosswalk. We waited for a high-pitched snowmobile to pass and then we made our way toward a tiny park with a huge Christmas tree. Jóla joined us by bounding over the street as though gravity was optional.

Under the darkened skies, the Christmas tree's blinding white lights turned my eyes into slits. The brightness seemed like overkill. I had to look away to keep my eyes from frying.

Turning to the road, I waited for an open sleigh. In Tinseltown, vacant sleigh taxis displayed a blinking green light, while occupied sleighs blinked red. Shaking my head, I watched three red-light sleighs pass in a row.

"Ruprecht, look," Marley whispered. She was facing the Christmas tree, her back to the road.

"I know," I said, eyes on the traffic. "The lights are a little much."

"No, Ruprecht," she said, pointing up at the tree. "Look between the lights."

I turned around and held my forearm above my eyes, straining to look at the tree. At first I only saw white lights. Among the intensely bright bulbs, here and there, duller lights served as decorative accents.

But then I saw it. My breath caught in my throat.

The duller white lights were no decorations—they were

pairs of eyes glowing out from the dark portions of the tree.

The white ovals moved in unison, sliding down the tree between the brighter lights. It was like they were all part of the same organism, like they were being controlled by some unseen force.

As they slinked downward, the individual shapes revealed themselves. They were black shadows resembling poorly drawn children. They were the Yule Kids.

The shadows slipped noiselessly to the ground, paused for a moment, and then scattered in the blink of an eye.

One of them zipped past Jóla, immediately engaging her predatory impulses. The giant cat whipped around, but another Yule Kid glided behind her and yanked on her tail. Jóla hissed and bounded after the fleeing shadows like she was chasing supernatural rats.

Five more shadows closed in on us from every angle. I looked helplessly at the completely still Halls of Justice. All the cops in Tinseltown were just across the street, but they might as well have been miles away.

The shadows' white eyes were angled as if expressing glee. They had us, and they knew it. I heard eerie childlike laughter. It sounded distorted and hollow, like it was coming from another dimension.

I had to do something. Anything.

"AAAAAH!" I yelled as I ran straight for one of the shadows and into the street. The shadow blipped away as I rammed through what felt like a cloud of icy fog. The coldness of the Yule Kid took my breath away and sent a wave of nausea rippling through my stomach.

A wall of Yule Kids swarmed toward me, inking out my view of the street and the Halls of Justice beyond. They were forcing me back toward the park.

Marley, by my side, stated the obvious: "There's too many, Ruprecht."

Then behind me, the sound of bone-rattling laughter. It sounded like winter boots stomping on broken ornaments. I knew who it was before my eyes could confirm it.

"Grýla," I said as I turned around.

She smiled with a face incapable of kindness. She was strikingly tall and moved with the elegant, assured movements of a skilled assassin. She wore a long gray robe with black trim. Her white hair sprung out in clumps from beneath a gray hood.

She wielded a staff like my mom's, but hers had a hollow upside-down Christmas star at the top with a purple flame flickering within.

Beside Grýla stood Pickwick the goblin. He frowned at me.

"Sorry, Mr. Krampus," he said with a shrug. "I had to give you up. Don't take it personally, it's just business."

"Get out of here, goblin," growled Grýla. She reached down to hand him a stack of chestnuts. The goblin flipped through the stack and inhaled the crisp scent of money.

With a tip of his cap, he bounded off, leap-frogging over cars and Townies, then onto a rooftop and out of sight.

"Hello, *krampus*." Grýla's long, spidery fingers curled menacingly around her staff. "I'm surprised the cops let you walk free. But all the better for me."

The Yule Kids closed in. Marley floated in closer.

"We should have a talk," sneered Grýla. "But first, I have some street cleaning to do." This provoked more unearthly laughter from the Yule Kids.

Grýla reached down and picked up a glass lantern that I hadn't noticed before. She pointed her staff at Marley.

My best friend looked at me with fear as a streak of purple lightning shot out from the upside-down star to engulf her entirely. I gasped as the dancing purple electricity zapped inside the lantern, Marley included.

The lantern now pulsed with a squirming gray flame. From somewhere deep inside it, I could hear the faint echoes of Marley calling for help. It all happened too fast. There was nothing I could do.

Grýla and the Yule Kids moved closer. The witch pointed her staff at me and blasted out another streak of purple.

I watched, helpless, as the street came up to greet me and the world went black.

When I came to, I found myself in a metal kennel in a brightly lit room. My head felt like a gift box that had been ripped open, emptied, and tossed aside.

Squinting through the lights, I flinched when Grýla came into focus on the other side of the cold, metal bars.

From a throne-like desk chair, she stared back at me without feeling. A bank of television monitors blinked and fizzled behind her. They appeared to show interior and exterior security camera feeds.

Above the monitors were the words "Illur Enterprises," along with the corporation's logo: the same upside-down star from Grýla's staff.

The monitors took up most of the wall opposite me, while durable-looking lockers and drawers lined both sides of the room. A large metal door to my right appeared to be the only way in or out.

It didn't take a master sleuth to deduce that I was somewhere within Grýla's headquarters, the soaring skyscraper on the western edge of Tinseltown.

How long had I been out? My head drumming, I searched the monitors for the time, but had no luck.

"Don't worry," said the glaring witch. "The headache should fade away in a couple of days."

Despite how I felt, I didn't want to appear rattled. Slowly, I reached into my pocket and noted with relief that she hadn't emptied them. I pulled out a candy cane and gently tore open the wrapper.

Looking at the witch with mild interest, I stuck the cane in my cheek.

"Where's the snow globe?" she asked. I appreciated her directness.

"Your guess is as good as mine," I said.

"Humbug," she said.

"There's no need for bad language," I teased.

She used her black-booted feet to pull herself and the wheeled desk chair closer.

"Do you have any idea how many chestnuts I can get for the snow globe?" she snapped. "With that kind of cash, I could take over Tinseltown for keeps."

I shrugged my shoulders. This seemed to aggravate her further.

"Your life is worth humbug to me on a good day!" she said through gritted teeth. "So imagine how little you matter when you're the only one standing between me and a sleighful of chestnuts."

Leaning back on the ground, I stretched out my legs and crossed my hooves in front of me. "You seem awfully confident that I have the snow globe. Which means you share the goblin's

wild idea that I'm the jollifier."

"Yes, you little devil," she said. "The goblin tipped me off. I paid him for the information so I could claim sole ownership of the globe."

"Surely the Yule Kids reported two krampuses at the scene of the first jollification," I said. "How do you know I was the one who did it? How do you know the goblin didn't set me up for a chestnut payday?"

The witch scowled and exhaled through her nose. "I don't care if there was a whole litter of krampuses at the crime scene. You're the one from the Christmas Castle. Who else would have that kind of access to Santa's first toy? What do you take me for? Some kind of snow-brained fool?"

"I wouldn't say it out loud," I said, surprised at my fake courage.

She smirked, seeming a little impressed herself. "You cheeky demon. I don't need you to confirm what I already know. The goblin heard on the streets that you were finding your victims at the Pastel Pines Lodge and then arranging appointments for them to glimpse your daddy's first toy down in Tinseltown. The goblin learned you were staying at the lodge and even learned your room number. When I called the front desk, they informed me the room was registered to none other than Ruprecht Claus-Perchta."

My heart raced, but I tried to seem calm as I rolled the candy cane around in my mouth.

"Do you happen to remember what that room number was?" I figured it was worth a shot.

"Quit acting innocent," she sneered. "We called the room and even paid you a visit, but we've only been able to reach your little helper. The little tree elf."

I struggled to hold back a very strong urge to yell. *What is this elf up to, and why is he dragging me into it?*

Grýla rested her elbows on the arms of her chair and laced her fingers in front of her.

"Listen, Ruprecht," she said, adopting a false kindness. "I know what it's like to grow up against the grain. Your parents are committed to the bright side, but you don't have to be like them. It feels good to be naughty, doesn't it?"

My calm eyes took her in, but I said nothing. She scooted her chair closer and shifted slightly to the left. When she did, I could see some scattered chestnut stacks and jewels on the desk behind her.

"You have a knack for evildoing, I have to admit," she said with convincing sincerity. "And believe me, it takes one to know one. You stole your dad's most powerful object and then turned it on vulnerable elf tourists. If I'm being honest, it reminds me of me when I was your age..."

Grýla kept talking, but I stopped listening. I was too distracted by the ring of keys I had spotted among the cash and jewels on the desk behind her. One of those keys might open this kennel. I needed to get my claws on them.

The witch's long fingers rapped on the bars, snapping me out of my new fixation. "Did you hear what I said, kid? It's not every day that Tinseltown's top crime boss offers you an internship."

"In a weird way, I'm flattered," I said. And I was. Even if I'd never consider joining Grýla's world of crime, there were thousands of naughty Townies who'd jump at the chance.

"But first things first," she said. There was an added edge to her voice. "Where is the globe? Just hand it over, and I'll make you rich beyond your wildest krampus dreams. Working with me, you'll have endless opportunities to terrorize the elves of

Tinseltown, plus I'll have the money and power to keep the cops off your back for good."

"I'll think about it," I lied. "But I need to know something. What makes you so sure this globe is as valuable as you think it is?"

She leaned back in her chair. "You know perfectly well why it's so valuable. It comes with a story the elves can't resist—it jollifies them on the spot. It's a story the underground market won't be able to resist either. According to my team, it could demand as much as 640 million chestnuts on the black market. It's that powerful."

I whistled at the number, and I meant it. "But why so much?" I asked as innocently as I could. "I mean, it's supposedly just my dad's first toy. That makes it enough to jollify an elf here and there, but that doesn't seem worth all those chestnuts. What's the sales pitch?"

"There's no sales pitch needed. That snow globe sells itself. What rich Townie wouldn't want a perfect representation of all of the holiday nonsense consuming this town?"

My expression didn't change, and the witch rolled her eyes impatiently. "I mean, think about it: Your mom, a powerful forest witch, used her magic to turn your dad, a nobody human orphan, into an immortal icon capable of spanning the universe in a single night."

"I know my dad's story," I said. "But what does the globe have to do with it?"

She groaned peevishly. "Put it together, kid. Your mom fell in love with your dad, a have-nothing human named Nikolas, because of his goody-goody toymaking and his silly need to make children happy. The snow globe is your dad's first toy, made with snow from the Laughing Valley's first snowfall the year he met your mom. He was holding the snow globe when your mom transformed him into Santa Claus. And it was in that moment that all of this holiday hogwash began."

I struggled to maintain my neutral expression. Though I knew it was fake, the story did have a ring of truth to it.

Grýla scrutinized my face. "Is it starting to sink in? That snow globe is a pure distillation of holiday magic, and holiday magic is one of the most powerful—and valuable—things in the world. Especially in this town."

"And you believe all that?" I asked. "You don't seem like the type to buy into holiday magic and love and goodwill toward men and all that."

Grýla laughed. "The truth is, it doesn't matter if I believe it, as long as everyone else does. One of those believers is going to fork over enough chestnuts for me to own this city—cops, judges, and Governor Lucia included. With that kind of money, I wouldn't need this corporation to pretend I make an honest living. With that kind of money, I could be as naughty as I want, and there would be nothing anyone could do about it."

She gave me a grim smile. "Doesn't that sound nice? You can be right there at my side, just living your naughty krampus life. What do you say?"

I stared back at her and sucked idly on my candy cane. "I already told you," I said. "I'll think about it."

Her smile melted into an impatient grimace. "It's the most valuable object in Yuletopia, you fool! And you're using it to give elves migraines. You need to think *bigger.*"

Just then, a deep, throbbing alarm sounded and a red light flashed above the door. Grýla whipped around and scanned the monitors. They all seemed empty of movement.

She grabbed her staff and spoke into the upside-down star on top. "Possible security breach, unclear where. Get everyone out there to secure the perimeter."

Grýla stood up and then stooped down to glare at me with unnerving yellow-tinged eyes. "Suit yourself, you wretched goat. I have plenty of time to break you down. Right now, I need to make sure your kitty isn't outside poking around."

Grýla kicked the kennel on her way toward the exit. "So,

get comfortable and try to discover some sense in that furry head of yours."

As the door closed behind her, she addressed someone or someones on the other side: "Tomi, Naka—stay here and watch this door. That krampus has to learn to cooperate."

When the door clicked shut, I exhaled with relief. I could drop the act, for now, and focus on that shiny ring of keys on her desk. They offered only the faintest glimmer of possibility, but right now, I had to cherish every glimmer I had left.

I took a deep breath and shook the cage bars with all my might. Well, I tried to shake them. They wouldn't budge. I lowered my shoulder and lunged into the bars, but only succeeded in creating a bruise. The bars remained indifferent.

Then I took a new approach. I reached my claws toward the desk at every possible angle, trying to lengthen my arms through sheer willpower.

But it was no use. No matter how hard I strained, I still needed another sixteen inches to reach those keys. I even tried using my tail, but that was even less successful.

I lay down with exhaustion and shooed away creeping feelings of dread. Many times, especially after the poltergeist incident, I had imagined what jail might feel like. And now here I was with an answer: Far worse than I ever could have imagined.

I thought grimly of the many judgmental creatures in the North Pole, especially ones from the Christmas pageant who would be tickled to know that I was behind bars, exactly where they thought I belonged.

Eyes closed, I tried to clear my mind. If there was a way out of this jam, hopeless feelings would not help me find it.

Fumbling inside my pocket for another candy cane, my claw brushed past the tree elf's fruitcake from the Ice Hotel. My stomach grumbled in response.

"Thanks for the snack, Marley," I said to the empty room. "Wherever you are."

Reluctantly, I placed my dwindled candy cane back in its plastic wrapper, opened the top of the loaf's paper wrapping, and began picking at the stale brick.

Despite being crammed with nuts, candy, and fruit, the fruitcake somehow managed to be flavorless and dull. It was very bad, but sometimes very bad is better than nothing.

I picked at what I thought was a sharp slice of candy and realized I was fiddling with a thin piece of cardboard.

I sat up and pulled the remaining loaf out of the paper. There, between the loaf and the wrapper, was a shiny black business card.

This wasn't the elf's left-behind snack—it was a hiding place to keep a secret. And what better place to hide a secret than wrapped up with a fruitcake, where nobody would look on purpose. Nobody, that is, except desperate souls like me.

The card was black with white letters. Along with an icon of a crystal ball with antlers growing out of it, there were these words: "Rudy the Remarkable: Psychic Readings & More. 100% Discreet. 92 Blitzen Circle." In the corner, there was a little starburst with a message: "Ask about our self-storage rates!"

I flipped the card over to find a series of numbers jotted in black ink: 24-34-00-96.

I had no idea what all this meant, but it felt like a genuine clue with a capital C.

"Rudy the Remarkable," I said out loud. My mind buzzed. Why would an elf need a psychic? Was this reindeer an accomplice?

I puzzled through a variety of scenarios, each more absurd than the last.

My furious thinking screeched to a halt at the sound of tapping from one of the lockers lining the wall. It was barely audible, but it was persistent. I knew it immediately—it was Marley trying to get my attention.

What's my move? I thought. I had to get out of here. Marley needed me. And we had a new lead in our case. The keys were right there. My heart screamed with frustration—I was so close to freedom and a possible breakthrough in the hunt for a jollifier.

Placing the candy cane back in my mouth, I used my tongue to adjust it while I pondered the situation. Then it hit me like an avalanche: *I'm a krampus.*

I pushed my face between two bars. With a deep breath, I stretched my forked krampus tongue out of the kennel and onto Grýla's desk.

I grunted from the strain as my tongue moved around among the chestnuts and the jewels. I accidentally curled around a chestnut bill and winced at the bitter, germ-crawl-

ing taste. With a few more probes, my tongue found the ring of keys, wrapped around it, and slung them back toward the cage.

After one indulgent moment of tired, silent celebration, I tested each of the dozen keys in the kennel lock, one by one. As I did, a thought popped into my head that didn't occur to me often enough.

Under the right circumstances, I thought, *being a krampus sure did have its perks.*

CHAPTER NINE

SKYSCRAPER ESCAPE

fter unlocking my cell, I went through the keyring until I found the winner that opened the locker holding Marley's lantern.

I got her out and stopped to think. After a few seconds, the lantern shook impatiently in my claw.

"You're right, you're right," I whispered, looking around the room. "I'll get moving."

It felt good to be outside the kennel, but with guards on the other side of that door, it seemed I had traded in one jail cell for a slightly bigger one.

The monitors displayed various feeds from inside and outside the building, including some spots around Tinseltown.

The video from inside the tower showed mostly empty rooms, save for a few workers sweeping here or typing there. I had completely lost my sense of time, but based on the lack of activity in the building and the busy shopping crowds on the Tinseltown feeds, it must have been some time in the evening.

The Illur employees in the video feeds didn't strike me as particularly evil looking, even though they worked for Grýla. They just looked a little bored, and maybe a little sad. The lantern shook again to remind me that contemplating depressed workers wouldn't help us escape.

My eyes continued up over the monitors, along the wall, and up the ceiling. Fluorescent lights beamed down overhead. A flickering bulb added to my feelings of dread and uncertainty.

Beneath the fizzling bulb, my gaze stopped on a vent cover about ten feet up the wall. But ten feet was too high. Even if I stood on Grýla's chair and reached, I would still be short by a good three feet.

Clink clink clink. I tapped a claw nail thoughtfully on the lantern's rounded glass. I looked down at my sharp, furry claw and up at the wall separating me from the vent.

I allowed myself a silent chuckle. Once again, it was time to cash in on my natural-born krampushood.

With the lantern handle in my mouth, I walked over to the wall. I reached my right claw as a test, and sure enough, without breaking a sweat, my nails dug firmly into the drywall.

"Here we go, Marley," I said. "Wish us luck." The lantern rocked slightly in response.

I knew I had to work as quickly as I could in case the forthcoming racket grabbed someone's attention.

With a deep breath, I crunched my right claw further into the wall, reached up with my left, and did the same. After three clawed grips, I was within reach of the vent. Using my left claw, I pried open the edge of the vent cover and sent it clanging down across the floor.

I placed the lantern inside the duct, crawled in after, and panted quietly in the cramped metal confines. The lantern's gray flickering light provided dull illumination of the duct path ahead.

The door opened down below, and I stopped breathing. I could hear a voice say, "What the...?" but I wasn't about to wait around to hear more.

My knees and claws banged against the inside of the duct as I pushed the lantern in front of me. I had no idea where this vent would take us, but it couldn't be worse than a kennel. Or so I hoped.

"'Let's start a detective agency,' we said," I muttered to Marley. "'We'll help some people, have a few laughs...'"

I thought I heard a sound behind me and I stopped to

listen. Nothing responded, so I continued scrambling forward.

Reaching an intersection, I blindly took a left. Up ahead, a vent let in dazzling bright green light.

When I got there, I shifted my hooves in front of me and kicked like a spooked horse. The vent plate popped off with two swift kicks. I dropped down and found myself in a carpeted corporate conference room with a long table and chairs. One of the walls was completely made of glass, beyond which stunning sheets of green aurora borealis shifted and swayed in the night sky.

Briefly overcome with delight, I noted the shades of bright purple and blue pulsing in along the edges. This wasn't any old aurora borealis. These were my mom's protective spells surrounding the building.

She was here to find me. But not if I found her first.

I heard yelling and fighting from somewhere outside, but the windows only showed the green illumination of my mom's witchcraft.

Far down below the magical green lights, Tinseltown winked and twinkled. To my left, the Christmas Castle shone on the horizon, the North Star gleaming brilliantly above it. This meant I was on the east side of the building, and from the looks of it, I was near the top of the skyscraper, about 35 stories high.

"Think, Ruprecht, think," I muttered to myself. I ran through the room and the green lights grew brighter. Then, it occurred to me: The lights would be their brightest nearest their source—my mom. If I could follow the brightness, I could find her.

Sprinting into the next identical room, I could see a figure outside the window, but it wasn't my mom. It was Grýla. She was zipping past on a broom made of dead, gnarled wood. She held her pentagram staff above her head and was zapping purple beams into the night.

I squinted from the bright purple light and tried to see where her shots were headed. My attention shifted to a flash of red streaking across the window.

The streak paused to reveal my mom, her back to me, flying on her own broom of birch and hazel. Yule Kids swarmed at a distance, as powerful bursts of green energy surged out of my mom's staff. Each streaking blast left a sheet of aurora borealis in its wake.

Grýla soared into view, facing me and dodging my mom's

attacks. My mom was trying to strike Grýla's staff, which was likely the source of her magical power.

Just as this thought crossed my mind, Grýla's upside-down star shot a surging flash of purple lightning directly at my mom.

With incredible dexterity, my mom streaked out of the blast's path. The burst of purple continued rocketing toward me and the wall-length window between us. I hit the ground as glass exploded with a deafening boom.

Freezing air and wind rushed in as shards showered down around me. I stood up and shook the glass bits from my fur and brushed it from the front of my jacket.

On the other side of the room, a groundhog peered into the doorway. He was wearing a polo shirt with Illur's pentagram logo on the breast pocket. His mouth gaped in shock at the hole in the side of the building and the thick layer of broken glass covering the carpet. He looked about as scared as I felt.

"Welcome to the party, pal," I said with a smile.

Mouth still open, the groundhog slowly backed away and out of sight.

I turned my attention to the skies. My hooves crunched

across the broken glass without a problem as I walked up to the blown out window. Holding my Santa hat in place so it wouldn't fly away, I peered over the edge of the building and up into the bright green sky.

The dueling witches were out of view, but I could hear them continuing their battle above me.

If I was going to get my mom's attention, I needed to get to the roof.

In the hallway, I found a door labeled "ROOFTOP ACCESS" with an icon of a staircase. The lantern shook in my claw, letting me know that, somehow, Marley could see the sign too.

I burst into the stairwell and clomped up the steps. Then, slowly, I opened the door and steadied it against a powerful high-altitude gust of wind.

When it calmed a little, I hunched down, scrambled behind a large metal chimney, and clung to a pipe. It was all I could do to keep from flying off into the night like a strange, furry kite.

The screeching wind filled my ears. Squinting my eyes, I realized it wasn't just the wind doing the screeching. Grýla was also joining in the high-pitched chorus as she hopped around zapping jagged purple beams into the glowing green sky.

In between blasts, she made wide-arching motions with her arms to conjure crescent-moon-shaped domes of light that crested across the sky. But the protective domes never lasted long—they were being attacked by my mom.

She zipped through the air, firing green lightning bolts of energy into the enchantment barrier, all while dodging Grýla's barrage and contending with Yule Kids cascading toward her like a cloud of shadowy bats.

Every once in a while, my mom would break through with a surging beam aimed at Grýla, but mostly she was kept on the defensive.

A particularly powerful blast from Grýla's staff forced my mom to abruptly change course and streak around the building. Her new position gave her an angle to see me for the first time.

"Ruprecht!" she yelled, halting immediately in her flight path. This one moment of hesitation was enough for Grýla to get my mom in her sights.

"Christmas is canceled, *Mrs. Claus!*" screeched Grýla. With a nails-on-stained-glass cackle, she aimed and fired her staff. The strike landed high on my mom's shoulder, sending her barrel-rolling backward through the sky.

"Mom!" I yelled, leaping out from my hiding spot. Grýla jumped back and stared at me like I had just burst out of her figgy pudding. "You sneaky devil," she said, as she aimed her staff at me.

Up in the sky, my mom had already recovered from the blow.

"That's Frau Perchta to you!" she roared. A rippling charge of green energy hurtled from high over my head and collided into Grýla. It was enough to freeze her on the spot, but it was too late—Grýla's staff had already fired.

I stood shocked and helpless as the purple energy blazed toward me.

At the last possible moment, I dove out of the beam's path. But I dove in the wrong direction. The icy air tore at my face as the lights of Tinseltown spread out before me. I was falling face-first off the building.

As the icy sidewalk grew closer, it occurred to me that despite all of my helpful krampus features, one thing I couldn't do was fly.

But my mom could.

I felt her arm swoop around my waist and pull me onto the broom behind her. Together we darted off through the sky, the lantern shaking excitedly in my claw.

I looked back to see the Yule Kids floating uncertainly around their leader. She remained on the roof, stiffer than a nutcracker thanks to my mom's magical charge.

In a rush of dark, frozen air, we dashed over Tinseltown. I gave my mom a hug of gratitude as the awesome green lights continued to ignite the sky behind us.

CHAPTER TEN

THE RED-NOSED PHONY

As we descended from the skies above Specterville, I spotted Jóla lying in the road in front of Marley's townhouse. She looked up, yawned, and stretched with her huge claws out in front of her.

My mom swooped down beside the big cat and I hopped off of the broom. As soon as my hooves touched down, I felt Jóla's purrs rumbling through the street. She nuzzled her head into my mom's side, and then mine.

"Yeah, yeah, yeah," I said, marveling at the gigantic white hairs the cat had left across my jacket. "It's good to see you too."

"Let's go inside, Ruprecht," said my mom. "I don't like doing magic out in the open like this, skyscraper battles

147

notwithstanding." She scratched under Jóla's chin and said, "I'll be back soon."

The white cat sat down to wait patiently as I ran up the steps with the glass lantern. My mom's magic opened the door as I approached it.

"Mr. Marley?" I called into the house as I ran to the dining room. But there was no response.

I placed the lantern on the table, and my mom entered the room behind me. She took a quick breath, gave her staff a slight twirl, and whispered, *"Exspiravit effugium lanterna."*

The lantern glowed green for a moment and Marley shot out like a gray firecracker. She floated before us, looking equal parts relieved and unsettled.

"Thank you, Frau Perchta!" she cried. "And thank you, Ruprecht. I'm so glad to get out of there."

Marley hugged my mom and then me, sending a shimmering feeling across my skin like a pleasantly mild electric shock.

The look of celebratory relief on Marley's face quickly dropped into a look of concern.

"I saw children in there…" she said, collecting her thoughts.

"It was all very hazy, but there was a group of kids trapped in some kind of interdimensional jail. They were all scared and confused. They told me they were the Yule Kids. They were naughty once, and Grýla has stolen their souls."

"The Yule Kids are actual kids?" I asked, confused.

"Yes," said Marley, forehead wrinkled with concern. "Grýla has them trapped against their will. The kids told me the witch has extracted their naughty urges to create those shadow ghouls that she uses to do her dirty work. Grýla has no use for the nice side of children. She just wants the naughty side. She keeps their nice side—their soul—imprisoned, while the naughty side does whatever evil thing she wants."

"We have to do something," I said. "Those kids deserve another chance. They have the right to be regular kids again. Mom—can you free them from that lantern like you freed Marley?"

My mom picked up the lantern and examined its every side.

"Unfortunately," she said, "we can't help them without being near their shadow forms. This lantern was merely a one-time portal. Grýla only enchanted it to imprison Marley. Now that she's free, the portal has closed and the lantern has returned to being a regular lantern."

She set it down and squeezed my shoulder. "Those children are split between realms, so we'll have to be very careful.

If we're too hasty, we might risk losing their souls forever. I'll speak with Governor Lucia and your dad—I'm sure we can figure out a way to set them free."

Shaking my head, I reached into my pocket for a badly needed candy cane. My claw brushed past the business card I found in the fruitcake.

"I almost forgot!" I yelled, startling my mom and Marley. I held the card so they could get a look at it. "I found a major clue wrapped beneath the fruitcake from the tree elf's hotel room."

"A psychic reindeer," marveled Marley. "Even after all these decades, Tinseltown never ceases to surprise."

I pulled out a chair, slumped down, and rested my head in my claws. It was all coming back to me.

"And I learned something else," I said. "According to Grýla, the jollifier is using a room at the Pastel Pines Lodge to lure tourist elves to sign up to get a glimpse of the snow globe. She said the room is registered under my name!"

"It's hard to trust Grýla's account of anything," said my mom. "But this is all possibly helpful evidence."

She gave me one of her trademark stern-but-gentle looks. "But it's possibly helpful evidence for the police to handle."

When I didn't respond, my mom crouched down and held my shoulders. She looked directly into my eyes.

"Listen, Ruprecht," she said. "I know you have a lot you'd like to prove, but you've already done so much to help. Please just tell the cops about your new clues and let them handle the jollification cases. And let me, Lucia, and your dad deal with Grýla."

She closed her eyes and murmured, "*Aurora borealis protego donom.*" As she whispered, green light burst in through the windows from outside.

"I've placed a spell on this house so that unwanted visitors can't enter. Nothing can hurt you if you stay within these walls. Nobody can come in that door unless you invite them inside. You and Marley need to stay here for now, Ruprecht."

I looked at Marley and then back at my mom. "I hear you, Mom," I said, which technically wasn't a lie.

All night long, I tried and failed to get some quality sleep. Every time I closed my eyes, I found myself plummeting helplessly toward the city from the top of Grýla's skyscraper. It was going to be a while before I got over that one.

I spent the next morning and afternoon trying to make up for my lack of sleep by resting and taking my mind off the case. But that wasn't happening either. There was too much going on. It felt like trying to relax in the middle of a tornado.

Now, it was 7 p.m. and we were in the Marleys' main room on the first floor, which they dryly referred to as a living room.

In the middle of the room stood a Christmas tree sporting a style from centuries past. It was adorned with walnuts, golden apples, and fire-lit candles suspended in midair by some spectral force.

Marley was poring over a book called *Soul Prisons: A History*, and I was glued to a telephone on a side table. I had been dialing the police station since daybreak, and I was starting to get on the iguana's nerves.

The yeti and the ice troll hadn't been in all day. According to the iguana, they were out following leads on the jollifications and otherwise dealing with the holiday rush of crime. Apparently, shopping isn't the only thing that picks up during the holidays.

I called again. This time, before the iguana could hang up on me, I asked him to jot down our new evidence and pass it on to Metoh and Schnee. I told him it was important. With an annoyed sigh, he agreed, and I gave him the updates.

"Pastel Pines? A psychic reindeer? The souls of naughty children?" he said. "Kid, you're either onto something or you're in bad need of a guidance counselor."

"That might be true either way," I said. "By the way, have

Metoh and Schnee found Bajazzo? Or is he still on the lam?" Marley floated in close to listen to his response.

"I'm not supposed to discuss case details," said the iguana, "but, between you and me, I think someone's got you hood-winked. We haven't been able to find anyone named Bajazzo anywhere. Whatever passport you saw was a fake."

"How many names does one elf need?" I asked, directing my question to Marley. She shook her head in disbelief.

"Forget it, Ruprecht. It's Tinseltown," said the iguana. "This city has more fake identities than Christmas wreaths. And, anyway, the Pastel Pines are outside TTPD's territory. Even if we wanted to, we couldn't send our cops to the lodge without a warrant from Governor Lucia. And that could take weeks."

"Not the good tidings I was hoping for," I said. "But if you could at least tell Metoh and Schnee what I've told you, we'd appreciate it."

He let me know he'd relay the message just as soon as he could. But soon wasn't good enough. I felt the clock ticking in my chest, and every tick felt like a heart murmur.

I could tell Marley felt it too. She had seemed shaken all day, and she was usually unshakable.

"How are you holding up?" I asked, as she returned to her book.

"Those kids were miserable, Ruprecht," she said. "They

thought they were being punished for being naughty, but I tried to tell them their punishment didn't fit their crimes. They don't deserve this."

"We'll find a way to get them out," I assured her. "I'm not sure how, but we will."

"Well, we can't do anything just sitting here," she said matter-of-factly. "There's a jollifier on the loose, and the souls of thirteen kids are hanging in the balance."

I twirled the reindeer's business card in my claw. "A good place to start might be that reindeer in the Bazaar District. This aurora borealis protection may not let bad creatures in, but that doesn't mean good creatures can't go out."

Through the front window I could see Jóla dozing on the roofs across the street. Her eyes were closed, but her ears were perked up and aimed at the house. She was in a half-asleep, half-ready position, primed to pounce into action at the first sound.

Marley and I crept up the stairs and toward my bedroom. She went invisible as I walked through the room, opened the window, and, as quietly as I could, clawed my way down the side of the building.

The brick was covered in a new layer of hoarfrost, but the slick surface was no match for sharp claws and a determined krampus.

I didn't enjoy defying my mom. I really didn't. But with the cops out of pocket, Marley and I had one remaining chance to get to the bottom of this jollification situation. Somehow, against all odds, that one chance sat with a reindeer psychic in the Bazaar District.

Marley remained invisible, but I knew she was right there with me as I slipped through back alleys, over wooden fences, and across side streets. I wanted to make it very difficult for Jóla to track us if she ever clued in to our absence.

After putting a comfortable distance between ourselves and the giant cat, I hailed a sleigh with a green light. It was pulled by a white horse with  a top-hatted mole in the driver's seat.

I asked the mole to take us to the Bazaar District. He nodded without looking at me, I crawled into the back seat, and the horse began trotting. Hunched down as far as I could, I tried my best to keep my face hidden from the general public.

Just north of Pagan Hill, the Bazaar District was a shopping borough for eccentric tastes. Shoppers looking for traditional gifts could shop on Santa Claus Lane in the CoZo. Shoppers looking for curios, oddities, and peculiar gifts know that the

Bazaar District is their destination for all things weird. Things like a psychic reindeer, for instance.

I paid the mole and we hopped out a few streets away from the reindeer's address. This would give us the chance to check out the area and make sure there were no holiday surprises lurking in the shadows.

My eyes darted and my nerves rattled as we made our way down a slick cobblestone street. The evening crowd was thinner here away from the city center, but there were plenty of eyeballs left to peer at the krampus kid hoofing nervously through their neighborhood.

"Do krampuses have a sweet tooth?" It was a warthog in a cart selling candied almonds. Avoiding eye contact, I declined and kept moving.

Following the street numbers down Blitzen Circle, I found myself in front of a ramshackle brownstone townhouse draped in pastel holiday lights. A large neon sign hung above the front door. It had an image of a Santa outfit with the words "Rudy the Remarkable's Psychic Readings, Costumes & More!"

The sign was off, but beneath it a smaller neon sign buzzed. It featured the same crystal ball with antlers from the business card, along with an arrow pointing down to the basement. Beneath the crystal ball were the words "Walk-ins Welcome (I've been expecting you)."

Along with the neon signs, smaller cardboard notices peppered the front of the building and detailed the "& More" part of the business's name. They advertised a variety of side services and products, including magic tricks, self-storage, and even printing.

"Wow," I whispered to my invisible friend through the side of my mouth. "This guy does it all."

"Maybe that's why they call him 'remarkable,'" Marley whispered back.

I walked down the few steps to a damp basement doorway. I knocked and I waited.

Eventually, hooves clicked on the other side of the door. They grew louder, then stopped, and the door slat opened abruptly. A big brown eye eyeballed me from within.

"Sorry, kid," the eyeball said. "To get a psychic reading, you'll need a permission slip from a parent or guardian."

"It will only be a minute," I said. The eyeball didn't respond, so I thoughtfully tapped my candy cane on one of my canine teeth. "Don't make me huff and puff…You don't want an angry krampus on your case, now do you?"

The eyeball muttered to itself. "I need to find a new neighborhood." Then, to me, it said, "I see all sorts of creatures in this place. A juvie krampus doesn't do much to move the fear needle."

"I brought chestnuts," I said. Before I could finish the "nuts" syllable, the door slat had closed and the door had opened.

As I suspected, the eyeball belonged to a reindeer. He wore a crisp white suit with a red silk tie. He was not one of the enormous reindeer that stand on all fours like the ones that pull my dad's sleigh. This reindeer stood on two hooves with antlers that added considerable altitude to an already tall frame.

At the end of his face glowed a bright, slightly flickering red nose.

Invisible Marley whispered in my ear: "The nose is fake. Battery operated."

"Thanks, Marley," I whispered, "I may not be the best detective, but I had that one figured out."

"What did you say?" said the reindeer.

"Nothing," I said. "I just have a few questions and I'll be on my way."

We were in a black-painted room with small dots of multicolored light scattered across the walls. Each light pulsed at its own frequency, changing from red to green to blue. It felt like I was in some sort of holiday-themed deep space.

In the middle of the room was a small round table with a white tablecloth. On top of the table, a crystal ball pulsed in colors mirroring those across the wall. The reindeer tapped a chair on one side of the table, telling me to sit down. He sat in a larger chair on the other side.

The reindeer closed his eyes and touched a hoof to each side of his nose. The room's pulsing colors danced and rambled across his white suit. He hummed eerily and then opened both eyes, as if waking abruptly from a deep slumber.

"The spirits are requesting chestnuts," he declared. Somewhere nearby, I heard Marley scoff at the mention of spirits. This caused the reindeer to cringe and look around the room. "Did you hear that?" he asked.

I sighed and placed a twenty-chestnut bill on the table. "Listen, Rudy," I said. "It is 'Rudy,' isn't it?"

The reindeer took the bill and slipped it inside his suit jacket.

"Actually," he said, "my name is Ren. 'Rudy the Remarkable' is my stage name. Some tourist elves from faraway places come here thinking I'm the real Rudolph, and I don't spoil it for them. You, on the other hand, are clearly not a tourist elf."

"Did the spirits tell you that?" I asked, with a not-too-subtle eye roll.

Suddenly, the lights surrounding us dimmed to blackness and the crystal ball flared with a rainbow burst of light.

"Shh…" said the reindeer, holding a hoof in front of pursed lips. "The spirits have something to say."

Marley whispered in my ear: "This guy is phonier than a shopping mall Santa. There's a pedal mechanism under his

chair. He's pressing it with his hoof to control the lights and the crystal ball."

"The spirits!" yelled the reindeer with dramatic enthusiasm. "The spirits tell me you're here because of a child! A human child whom you'd like to carry away in a basket!"

"The spirits must be having an off day," I said. "I'm not here because of a child. I'm here because of an elf—an adult elf."

"Whoa ho ho!" said the reindeer, as if he had won an argument. "A human child is about the same size as an adult elf. The spirits are on the right track!"

"Marley," I said. "This could go on forever. Let's put an end to these reindeer games."

The light inside the crystal ball went dark in a snap. I could hear the reindeer stamping down on the foot pedal. "What is happening?" he muttered.

Marley's flowing white hair filled the ball. She was facing the reindeer and cackling menacingly: "Hey Ren!" she cried. "It's me, an authentic spirit!"

The reindeer screamed and jumped out of his chair. His frantic movement sent his red plastic battery-operated nose skittering across the floor.

The lights flipped on and Marley vanished from the ball to appear beside me.

"Easy, buddy," I said, approaching the reindeer cowering

in the corner. "We thought you might be comfortable around spirits. It is your profession, after all."

"It's all a scam!" cried the reindeer. "I'm sorry! I repent! Are you the Ghost of Christmas Future? Or Christmas Past? Are you here to teach me a lesson?"

"No," said Marley with a mischievous smile, "but I can give your business card to my dad if you'd like."

"Just relax, Ren," I said. "We're not trying to teach you anything. Like I said: We just have a few questions. And you can keep the chestnuts."

This last part seemed to calm the reindeer considerably. He stood up and brushed off his suit.

"Please, just ask your questions," he said as he gathered his nose from the ground.

"Do you know a small tree elf, specifically a ponderosa tree elf? He's a couple heads shorter than me, goes around in an acorn backpack."

"An acorn backpack?" asked the reindeer, touching his hoof to his chin. "Ah, yes. An elf came in a couple weeks ago to buy an acorn backpack from me, along with some costumes and other things. He was on a bit of a shopping spree. Not uncommon this time of year."

"Costumes?" I asked.

I must have had a funny expression, because the reindeer

took a step back and responded slowly.

"He bought a teddy bear bandleader costume, a tree elf costume, and a state-of-the-art mechanical krampus costume... built with stilts so an elf can operate it from within. All of my costumes come in elf-friendly variations. If they didn't, I'd lose a lot of business."

Ren caught Marley and I sharing a grim look.

"*Stilts*," I said, shaking my head. "That's why the krampus had a limp."

"Wait a minute," said Ren. "What's going on here?"

"Don't worry about it," I said, crinkling the wrapper on a fresh candy cane. "You can ask your spirits about it after we leave. Now, you seem to have a lot of side businesses going on under one roof. Did the elf happen to take you up on your '& More' offerings?"

"Hey, it's a tough economy." The reindeer sounded a little defensive. "Psychic readings don't pay all the bills. But yes, along with the costumes, the elf picked up some smoke bombs and rented a storage unit. Come to think of it, he was a very good customer."

"A good customer," I said. "But not such a good citizen. Do you remember what he was wearing when he came in, Ren?"

"I was more focused on his chestnuts than his outfit," said the reindeer. "But I do remember he was wearing a miner's hat—one of those hard hats with a light on it."

Marley and I shared another look. This reindeer had more clues than a scavenger hunt.

I rooted around in my pocket and pulled out the Rudy the Remarkable business card. "One last thing we'll bother you with, Ren. Can you take us to the elf's storage unit?"

"I mean, you can look at the outside of the locker," said the reindeer. "But I don't have his combination."

"I can take care of that," I said, holding up the card with numbers.

"Like I said," said the reindeer. "He was a very well-paying client. It wouldn't be right to give up his storage unit...without, you know..."

This reindeer was about as subtle as a blizzard. I handed him a bill with Frosty's face on it.

Ren nodded, folded the money neatly, and slid it into his pocket.

We followed him down a flight of stairs into a musty room beneath the basement that smelled something like a hobgoblin's underwear drawer.

"Sorry about the smell," said Ren. "This subbasement is connected to the Tinseltown sewer system. My mortgage is sky-high—I have to make money off every millimeter of this place if I'm going to squeak by."

A row of more than a dozen red lockers were built into a wall of wet underground stone. Across from the lockers was only darkness. Distant, echoing drips indicated the beginning of a long tunnel.

"He has locker 12," said Ren, turning his back to us. "I'll look away while you look inside, but make it quick."

After going through the numbers, the door popped open. I coughed as an overwhelming waft of ponderosa-pine-tree scent billowed into my face. It was coming from tree-shaped air fresheners that are supposed to hang from the rearview mirror of a sleigh, car, or snowmobile.

The smell was identical to the elf's scent when he'd quivered his way up the stairs and into Marley's study. He'd been faking it.

Marley reached in and pulled out a miner's hat with a light at the front, just as Ren described. She flicked the light's switch, and for a moment, a faint beam illuminated the dripping sewer tunnels stretching out behind us. But after a few sputters, the light died out.

When Marley removed the miner's hat, she'd uncovered a brochure beneath. I picked it up and read it aloud. It was a promotional brochure for the Pastel Pines

Lodge—the same place that Grýla had mentioned.

The brochure advertised a ritzy-looking treehouse resort as a popular destination for rural elves looking for a festively exotic place to stay.

Apparently, a main selling point was the lodge's train station providing guests access to a variety of popular tourist destinations in Tinseltown, the North Pole, and beyond.

Marley filled the miner's hat with the ponderosa air fresheners. I placed the brochure in my jacket's inside pocket.

As Ren fiddled with the locker to reset the combination, Marley and I took a few steps toward the darkness of the city's sewer system. Tinseltown's underbelly.

"I have a funny feeling, Marley," I said. "And it's telling me that if we were to follow this tunnel, we could work our way to a sewer hole by the tree line of Belsnickel Park on the east side of the Glacé Bridge."

"That's very specific," said Ren, still working on the locker.

"Too bad those tunnels are too dark to see three inches in front of our faces," said Marley. "Which is why our jollifier wore a miner's hat." She tried the switch on the hat's light, but it didn't respond.

"Oh, well," said Ren. "Guess you'd better go home."

The reindeer turned from the locker and walked over to join us. When he did, the light from his nose cast an eerie red glow down the yawning sewer tunnel.

In unison, Marley and I looked up at the supposedly psychic red-nosed reindeer.

"Ren, I'm not sure if you could see this one coming," I said. "But we're going to need you to guide us with that bright red nose of yours."

CHAPTER ELEVEN

THE THIRD JOLLIFICATION

The sky was frozen ink when I crawled out of the sewer near Belsnickel Park. The full moon was big and bright enough to get your attention, even if you had a lot going on.

Marley and I looked down at the rectangular sewer opening. Ren and his red nose beamed up from within.

Navigating the underground network of sewer tunnels was a little tricky, but between Ren's nose and Marley periodically floating above ground to verify our location, we made the journey to Belsnickel Park in just about 45 minutes.

That gave us plenty of time to fill the reindeer in on all the particulars. Now, as we said our goodbyes, he promised to call the cops with his story, and to let us know if the elf showed up.

In the end, Ren turned out to be very cooperative, but all those chestnuts may have had something to do with it.

As the reindeer began hoofing it home, Marley and I turned around to face the Glacé Bridge, shining silvery in the moonlight.

Before we crossed the bridge, we surveyed the one-time crime scene. The cops had cleared out, apparently deciding the area no longer held any clues.

The jollification played back like a movie in my mind, but now there was a new ending. After that unnerving laugh, the krampus-disguised elf had limped across the street, deployed a smoke bomb, jumped out of the costume, and scrambled into the sewers, costume in hand.

A full-grown krampus could never fit down a sewer hole. But if I could fit, an elf wouldn't even have to suck in his gut.

The cops probably never considered the possibility. Marley and I certainly didn't. Not until Ren's nose illuminated the sewer tunnels and shined some light on our case in the process.

As we crossed the Glacé in silence, Marley floated backward so she could face me. The scent of ponderosas wafted out from the miner's hat that she held in front of her.

"So, now we know some 'whats' and 'wheres,' but we're still missing the 'why,'" she mused. "We know that he's luring elves

at the Pastel Pines Lodge. It's a place filled with elf tourists, and, conveniently, is outside of TTPD's jurisdiction. We know the elf is committing his crimes in Tinseltown to frame you, and then retreating to the Pastel Pines, where the cops can't reach him. Then, as a go-between, he's using Ren's locker to stash costumes and other evidence before and after his jollifications."

Marley propped a hand on her hip. "But why? Why go through all that trouble to frame you? What does that little pipsqueak have against a random krampus kid from the North Pole?"

"Yes, 'Why?' is an excellent question," I said. "And also, 'Who?' Who is he really and what is he trying to hide? He's not a genuine ponderosa elf, that's for sure. He's some other kind of elf dressed in a ponderosa elf's costume and coating himself in ponderosa scent. And, apparently, he enjoys roleplaying as a teddy bear bandleader in his spare time."

We kept walking, lost in a maze of puzzling clues. The fake psychic helped confirm the fake ponderosa elf was also a fake krampus. But he was the real jollifier. My gears were cranking so hard, it made my head throb.

Consumed by thought, the city disappeared around me. Eventually, I was jarred out of my brooding trance by Marley urgently whispering my name.

I had almost waltzed right past Marley's alley. Back on track, I ducked in behind her and clawed my way up the side of her house.

Once inside, it felt comforting to be off the Tinseltown streets and under the protection of my mom's magic.

I quietly descended the stairs and peeked through the drapes of the front window. Jóla was sleeping peacefully on the rooftop across the street, her white fur blending in perfectly with the surrounding snow. If not for her gently twitching tail, I might not have seen her at all.

With a pot of cider heating in the kitchen, Marley and I retreated to her parlor to discuss our situation.

We were confident that the elf, whatever his real name might be, was the culprit. But we didn't know if he was acting alone. And we didn't know if he was out there stalking around as a tree elf, a krampus, or a teddy bear bandleader. Somehow that last one was the most intimidating.

Marley began comparing the *Tinseltown Herald's* latest reporting with a book filled with maps of Tinseltown's railroads and sewer lines. I decided to make myself useful by checking in with our penguin friends at the Ice Hotel.

A tired-sounding penguin told me the tree elf with an acorn backpack had not checked back in. With something approaching annoyance, the penguin further confirmed that neither a teddy bear bandleader nor a krampus had checked in either.

To help our deep thinking, I put a jazz percussion record on Marley's phonograph. My mind cleared slightly as the parump-a-pum-pumming filled the parlor. I always liked drums. A drum was clear and straightforward, and it always told the truth, unlike certain former clients of mine.

"The first jollification was in the Bazaar District," said Marley, pointing into her book. "And the second was further southeast on Pagan Hill. The path from Ren's to Belsnickel Park to the jollification on Pagan Hill forms a zigzag heading south. If that's the beginning of a pattern, I would wager the next jollification will happen in the neighborhood southwest of Pagan Hill—"

Before either of us could say "Specterville," a wild cry sounded from the foyer: "Krampus! Elf! Snow globe!"

I jumped out of my seat, and Marley nearly shot through the ceiling.

From the front door, the panicked semi-transparent head of a young boy ghost poked into Marley's home. It was a neighbor ghost named Danny. I got up and turned off the banging percussion of the jazz record.

Marley floated to the head. "What's going on, Danny?"

"The big cat is chasing a krampus! I need to come in, but I can't!" cried the ghost. "Something is blocking me from coming in—"

His cries were cut off by the sound of jolly laughter. A little too jolly for comfort.

Marley and I looked at each other, and I walked up to the door. I opened it and Danny rushed inside. Now that he was invited, the protective spell allowed him in.

The source of the laughter was on the porch—it was a giggling elf, hunched over and stumbling toward me.

This elf needed help. "Come in, please! You're invited in!" I yelled frantically, trying to break the spell.

It was a tree elf in a threadbare outfit of bark and green felt. He wore a pointed hat and white-and-green-striped sleeves and leggings. His snow-white beard fell down from his chin in a point. It jiggled slightly as he giggled, struggling to speak.

"A krampus...hee hee...tried to jollify me...ho ho...with this...ha ha ha!"

The elf staggered into Marley's house and crammed a snow globe into my chest, tittering, "It's so magical! It's so much magic!"

I grabbed the globe as the elf collapsed in a giggle fit on the floor of Marley's foyer. Marley closed the door, and I quickly

set the snow globe on a side table. We both rushed down to the hysterical elf.

"Breathe easy," I said, holding his head. "Nice and easy breaths. In, out. In, out."

Despite my coaching, the elf couldn't breathe. Rolls of laughter kept coming. They were too much to control.

"He tried to jollify me in front of your house…hee hee hee… Santa made this snow globe as his first toy…ha ha ha ha…I just wanted a glimpse…ho ho ho…I can't take it!"

"Marley—do you have any coal? This elf is about to lose it."

"I'll check the fireplace!" she said, darting across the room.

"Danny," I said, glancing up at the ghost floating near the door. "What happened out there?"

"The big cat scared the krampus," he said quietly. "The krampus dropped the snow globe and ran away."

Marley glided over with a chunk of coal from the fireplace and waved it under the elf's nose. The elf groaned with eyes clamped shut. He was losing consciousness.

"Did the big cat catch the krampus?" I asked.

"No," said Danny. "The krampus disappeared in a cloud of smoke. The cat kept running down the road and out of sight."

"Jóla could probably hear the elf running down the sewer," I said to Marley.

"Which direction was the cat heading, Danny?" Marley

asked, eyes on the elf.

"Um," said Danny, scratching the side of his head. "I'm not very good with directions…"

Suddenly, the elf opened his eyes with a fit of wheezing laughter. "Northwest!" he cackled. "The kitty went northwest!"

"Relax, pal," I said to the elf. "We're going to get you to the hospital. You're going to be just fine."

"Just fine!" wheezed the elf in a grimly jolly way. "Everything is just fine!"

I could feel the elf slipping away from us into a jollified slumber. But before that happened, I needed information.

"Who invited you here to see the globe? Do you remember who they were and where you met them?"

"It was a little bear!" The elf was chortling, as if remembering a beloved joke. "A little bandleader bear in Pastel Pines Lodge, room 403! He sent me to Specterville to behold Santa's first toy! And then…there was a krampus!"

The elf pointed at my face, wide-eyed, as if he had just noticed me for the first time.

Then he let loose a blood-curdling scream that was enough to scare the ghosts of Specterville back to life.

The elf's tongue came out of his mouth, and his eyes turned bright white. They began blinking in an alternating rhythm. He was jollified.

In stunned silence, we delicately lifted the elf and carried him to the sofa in Marley's parlor.

"Danny, are you ready to be a hero?" Marley floated over to the young ghost. "The cops seem to be avoiding us, but they'll surely listen to you. Can you hurry as fast as you can to the Halls of Justice and let them know what happened?"

Danny gave a salute and disappeared in a blink.

With one claw on my forehead, I picked up the snow globe. I gasped and yelled, "Marley!"

"What is it?" she said, floating to my side.

I spun the globe in my claws. Inside, surrounded by flurrying snowflakes, was a humble shack between two evergreens. It was a normal-looking, run-of-the-mill snow globe. But it was one that I knew very well.

"It's not bad," said Marley, "but it doesn't seem like the work of a master toymaker."

"You're exactly right, Marley," I said. "It's not even the work of an adult."

I flipped the snow globe over. There was a name scrawled across the bottom in uneven letters. The name was Ruprecht.

"This isn't Santa's first toy," I said. "It's *my* first toy. My dad helped me make it when I was six years old."

CHAPTER TWELVE

THE PASTEL PINES

I shook the globe. The water gushed and the snowflakes whirled. From the globe's curved glass, my upside-down reflection stared back.

This naughty elf was really turning the screws. Not only had he been using my childhood snow globe as a weapon, but he had also brought the crime scene to my front door. He wanted me tossed in the Cooler, and he didn't care how many elves it took to get me there.

The jollified elf's head was slumped to the side in a twinkly eyed nap. His chest heaved up and down, and every exhale was accompanied by a little giggle. Though his breathing was steady, this elf was completely unconscious.

I set the snow globe on the side table and looked through the elf's pockets for clues.

In addition to his Pastel Pines Lodge key card, a handful of chestnuts, some licorice, and spare shoe bells, I found a snowplow operator's license. His name was Nutmeg and he lived on the distant Mistletoe Mountain.

"Poor Nutmeg," said Marley, continuing the coal treatment. "He probably wanted a little break from plowing snow on Mistletoe Mountain. He buys a vacation package for the Pastel Pines Lodge, he falls for a completely made-up story about Santa's first toy, and he ends up a jollified mess."

"A fake story with real consequences," I said, as I gently returned the elf's items to his pockets. "I don't think anything our former client told us was on the level. The buzzitrol, the krampus business partner, his job as a professional thief—he just spun it all out of thin air."

"Even though it's all made up, it will take some time to unravel this story with the cops," said Marley. "We have so much evidence against Bajazzo, or whoever he is, and Ren can back us up. But when the cops get here, they'll want us to stick around and answer questions for who knows how long."

"You're right," I said. "And even if we're able to convince Schnee that we know what we're talking about, by then it might be too late. For all we know, the jollifier is already halfway to

Swirlwind Bay dressed like a teddy bear bandleader."

I began pacing through the room, clomping on the hardwood floor beside the sofa.

"If we're going to figure out what's going on, I need to go to the Pastel Pines Lodge and at least see what I can find," I said. "It could be our last chance to crack this case, find the elf, and drop him down the chimney of the Tinseltown Halls of Justice."

Marley nodded. "OK, Ruprecht," she said. "I'll wait here for the cops and the paramedics to come. Should we let your mom know what's going on?"

"I'll call her from the lodge," I said. "She'll try to convince me not to go, and we don't have that kind of time to waste."

"Call me as soon as you find anything, and I'll let you know what I learn from the cops," said Marley.

As I packed the snow globe into a leather satchel and slung it around my shoulder, I caught Marley looking at me with a grave expression. It was mostly determination, but there was a dash of fear as well.

"Be careful out there, Ruprecht," she said. "That elf might be headed to the Pastel Pines Lodge, which means he might be on your train."

"Thanks, Marley," I said, trying to hide my own fear. But it was no use. She knew me too well. "Whatever happens, I'll see you on the other side."

Wailing sirens approached from a distant street as I bounded up the stairs and into my bedroom. After throwing on a hooded cloak, I climbed out the window.

It was after midnight, which made it Winter Solstice. It was the shortest day of the year and the eeriest time of night.

The full moon beamed above, and the snow and ice sparkled below. It might have been calming under other circumstances. But these weren't other circumstances.

With my cloak's hood casting my face in shadow, I stood waiting on the outdoor train platform at Specterville's Phantom Passage train terminal. I side-eyed the waiting phantoms and ghouls warily, many wearing hooded cloaks like me. But none of them were in krampus costumes, none of them were teddy bears, and none of them were elf-size.

With a commuter train arriving every 15 minutes, I didn't have to wait long for the boxy silver train to clank and clatter into the station.

At this hour, even in Specterville, there were plenty of seats to choose from. It was a westbound train with the Pastel Pines Lodge terminal serving as an early stop on its looping route along Yuletopia's western edge.

I kept my hooded face glued to the window and my back to the train as we gained speed. My ears were perked up, ready to alert me to anyone who walked down the aisle. But nobody did.

Soon, the city buildings gave way to smaller homes, and eventually to remote-looking cabins. After a few minutes, the city had been completely replaced by snowcapped trees.

The full moon was coming into its own and claiming much of the sky. But black clouds glowered on the sky's edges, creeping closer to the moon and threatening to snuff it out.

I rested my claw on my satchel as I stared out the window. It was hard to imagine that this simple trinket could cause so much trouble.

Somehow, the elf stole the snow globe from my bedroom bookshelf, where it had been for the past six years. He broke into the Christmas Castle to steal an innocent toy that my dad and I had created together in a fun, carefree afternoon.

And he didn't stop at stealing it. He used it to cause harm. It was as though he'd found a way to weaponize my childhood itself.

My ears popped as the train climbed in elevation. Now in dense forest, large pine branches surrounded the train and blocked out the moonlight. We had been swallowed by coal-black darkness, save for the dull light from the train's windows

casting a thin glow on the passing branches.

The trees ballooned in size as we climbed higher and higher. From the looks of it, we were now passing the midsections of trees that were 400–500 feet tall.

As we continued, the branches gradually transitioned from those of dark green pine to multicolored pastel evergreen needles of cotton candy pink, soft lavender, mint green, and icy blue. The famous Pastel Pines.

Even with a window between us, I was struck by their pungent, intoxicating scent. It smelled like someone had tossed Christmas trees, sugar cookies, and marshmallows in a blender and pulsed away.

The train began to slow as the wooden cabins of the Pastel Pines Lodge filled my window. They were built up and down the tree branches and across the trees' chunky bark.

Every window of every cabin was framed with pastel holiday lights, and every door displayed a pinecone wreath. While it wasn't my preferred decorative style, I could see why tourist elves would be drawn to this place.

I shuffled off the train with a small clawful of my fellow passengers. I kept my pace sluggish to blend in with the groggy crowd. At this hour, people in a hurry drew attention. And attention was the last thing on my Christmas list.

Our narrow train platform led us to the main lobby of the

Pastel Pines train terminal, a spacious building made entirely of light-brown wood. It was like a holiday cabin for giants.

Through the main doors of the terminal, the Pastel Pines Lodge spread out above me. The cabins and pathways were connected by wooden staircases and globular pastel elevators that looked like vintage Christmas ornaments.

Among a few guests milling about, most of whom were elves, I saw hotel clerk elves wearing white uniforms and puffy white winter hats that reflected the pastel colors in an eye-catching way.

I might have to chat up the staff later, I thought, but first I would find room 403 and possibly confront whatever elf, teddy bear, or krampus happened to open the door.

I quietly clomped up the stairs to the first level of cabins. My breath billowed out of my cloak's hood and around my head as I continued hoofing it up the gigantic pastel pine tree.

Reaching the third level, something bright caught my eye, and I turned around. It was the city skyline of Tinseltown, far down below past the train terminal.

Unwrapping a new candy cane, my eyes coasted beyond the twinkling city to the North Star burning brightly above the Christmas Castle.

Between dark and looming clouds, the brilliant star glowed like a monument to my childhood innocence. To a time when making a snow globe was just a fun, easygoing thing. When a snow globe was a little bit of magic, and nothing else.

With the candy cane rolling in my mouth, I completed my trek to the fourth level and to room 403.

I lowered my hood and placed an ear against the lavender door. Silence. The windows were shuttered with white drapes and revealed nothing.

With a deep breath, I gathered my courage to knock.

A twig snap from above grabbed my attention. I looked up just in time to see a light blue shape screaming with fury and hurtling toward me.

"I've got you, you jollifier! Don't even think about trying to escape!" the blue shape yelled. Before I could process what was happening, I found myself wrestling an elf.

"Pretty cheeky to come back in an upgraded krampus costume!" she yelled, as she dug her knees into my torso and tried to pull my head off.

With a grunt of effort, I rolled her off of me and held my claws up. "Please, stop!" I said, sitting on the ground. "I'm obviously a real krampus.

And I'm not a jollifier. You have the wrong guy."

"Then what is that?" The elf was pointing to the snow globe rolling on its side beside me. It had fallen out of my satchel during our scuffle.

"It's just a snow globe," I said, lungs heaving as I slowly stood up. "Just a plain old snow globe."

"That's not a plain old snow globe," she snapped. "That's the snow globe the *Tinseltown Herald* and HARK News are reporting as the suspected jollification weapon. Rumor says it's Santa's first toy."

I picked up the globe and, satisfied it was unharmed, held the bottom toward the elf. "Santa didn't make this toy," I said. "I made it. That's my name. Ruprecht."

As she examined the globe, I got my first good look at my attacker.

Her Pastel Pines Lodge nametag said her name was Snegurka. She had ink-black hair, glowing blue eyes, and ruddy cheeks. She wore one of the hotel clerk outfits I had seen on other workers, but hers was light blue with fluffy white trim. On her shoulder was a walkie-talkie. On her head was a light blue winter hat with a white ball at the top.

"I don't buy it," she said. "You could have just scribbled that on to throw off the cops. At first I thought there was an elf, a teddy bear, and a krampus all sharing the same room—but now I know you're a jollifier with many disguises."

"Tug my fur, knock on my horns—this isn't a costume." I turned around in a circle, making exaggerated expressions with my face to get the point across. "I mean, come on. If this is a costume, where's the zipper?"

The elf's shoulder walkie-talkie blared and a voice came through: "Sneg, is everything OK? Someone reported a commotion on level four. Over."

The little elf looked at me suspiciously as she squeezed the walkie-talkie and cocked her head to speak into it. "All clear, Starbeam. I'm just straightening a few things out. Over."

She walked up, stood on tiptoe, and poked my chest. Her azure eyes carefully scrutinized my krampusy details.

"OK," she said, almost disappointed. "You're real. But that doesn't mean you're not the jollifier."

"Snegurka, is it?" I asked, and she nodded. "My name is Ruprecht Claus-Perchta, and I have a story to tell you."

"Wait a minute—that's actually your real name?" she said, shocked. "I assumed that was an alias the jollifier used to disguise his identity when he booked the room. But that means your parents are…"

"I'll tell you everything, I promise," I said. "But first, a couple of questions. One: You said whoever was staying in 403 has split? And two: Do you have a key?"

"Yes and yes," she said. "He took off about 30 minutes ago in a teddy bear costume, and, duh. I'm a manager here—I have a key to all the rooms."

"I bet a nice luxury hotel like this has plenty of complimentary cocoa," I said, delivering my most trustworthy smile. "What do you say we go in and have a cup?"

Inside, I found myself in a rustic wood cabin with all the holiday touches to make an elf feel at ease. There was white plush furniture bathed in pastel light, a fire crackling spiritedly in the hearth, and an orange-cinnamon scent wafting through the air.

Snegurka sat across from me with a mug of cocoa. As I gave her the full lowdown, she sat there sipping, but she seemed too amped to enjoy it.

"That's some good detective work," she said. "On my end, in addition to him registering with what I thought was a fake name, I knew the elf was suspicious the moment he tried to pay me off to keep quiet about his comings and goings. I'm the hospitality manager of this hotel—he thought that if he could buy me off, he'd keep my team quiet too."

She took a rushed swallow of her cocoa and clinked her

mug onto the table. "Then tonight, I knocked on his door to confront him. He bowled me over wearing a teddy bear costume and ran away. When I searched through his room, I found everything I needed to confirm my suspicions—he is the jollifier."

"Hospitality manager, huh?" I smirked at the elf and sipped my own cocoa. "You have a funny way of welcoming visitors."

"I'm sorry about that," she said with a shrug. "I thought you were the elf coming back to collect the things he left behind."

Snegurka reached beneath the counter and held up a stuffed black garbage bag. Inside was an elaborate krampus costume, complete with stilts and arm extensions. Joining it was the ponderosa elf getup he wore when I first met him, including the pinecone belt and wig of elfin blond hair.

"The only thing that's not here is the acorn backpack," she said. "And he wasn't wearing it when he took off. So, he either got rid of it or stashed it somewhere else."

"You're not such a bad detective yourself," I said. "You ever think of becoming one?"

"All the time!" she cried with infectious enthusiasm. "And I'm not done yet."

She walked over to the small table beside the kitchenette and picked up a copy of the *Tinseltown Herald*.

"He circled the 9 a.m. train. It's the InterRealm Express, which will take him through Yuletopia, past Tinseltown and the North Pole, all the way to a freighter ship that sails to Ignorway."

I examined the paper, and she was right. In the bottom left corner of the page was a tourism ad for Ignorway with the headline, "It's not that bad, anymore!" The ad included a train schedule with the 9 a.m. InterRealm Express circled in red.

Ignorway is the pollution capital of the known universe. No one would go there on purpose…unless they were trying to hide from the known universe.

"He's out there somewhere, biding his time," she said, "but we know he'll be on that train in the morning. There's no way he's coming back here now that he knows I'm on to him."

"And the InterRealm Express only has one stop in Tinseltown," I said. "It's at Black Friday Forever, the biggest mall in the city. We need to get him off that train."

"This close to Christmas," considered Snegurka, "BFF is going to be overflowing with shoppers when the train pulls into that station."

"Which could be to our advantage," I said. I tore the page from the newspaper and folded it into my pocket. "Snegurka, we have some arrangements to make. Is there a phone we can use?"

"Yes," said the elf. "And call me Sneg. The Pinecone Conference Room is a few doors down. We can make calls from there."

"Let's go, Sneg," I said. "And thanks for the help." Then, with one hoof out the door, I turned around. "Why do you trust me?" I asked.

She shrugged. "Why wouldn't I?"

The elf raised a good question.

CHAPTER THIRTEEN

THE INTERREALM EXPRESS

It didn't take a crack detective to guess we were heading to a room designed like a huge pinecone. The Pinecone Conference Room was very on-brand for this hotel.

Sneg unlocked the mint-green pinecone's door and let us into an empty wood-paneled room equipped to fit a couple hundred visitors. She led me to a long table made from a single piece of pine.

We sat next to a device shaped like a raccoon's head in the center of the table. Sneg touched its nose, and a dial tone sounded.

"It's a speakerphone for conference calls," she said. "Out-of-town business elves get a kick out of it."

"Well, let's put this raccoon to work," I said as I reached across the table to snag a notepad and a pen shaped like a pine branch.

Of course, our first call was to Marley, and the three of us hatched a plan. I jotted down notes as we discussed, brainstormed, and diagrammed our next moves.

It was a whirlwind of excited conversation as we strategized our final steps to give Tinseltown a neatly wrapped Christmas gift of justice and clear my name once and for all.

We even came up with a plan to free the Yule Kids, but it was going to require the help of everyone in my family. With Sneg operating the raccoon head, we eventually patched my parents and all six of my sleepy siblings into the conference line.

After that call and a few others, I looked down at all the names in my notebook, and a thought crossed my mind.

The hardboiled detectives that Marley and I read about did one thing wrong: They rarely had enough help. Too often, they barreled into situations alone to accept all the punches, pain, and glory that went along with the job. They didn't share the risks, and they didn't share the rewards.

But not this detective. I felt no shame in knowing that I needed the support of my friends and family to succeed. It felt good to wholeheartedly embrace that fact.

And no matter how things changed as I got older, no matter

what kind of krampus I became, I hoped it was a feeling I would never lose.

I arrived alone at the Pastel Pines train station just before 9 a.m. The crowd was much thicker and livelier now, which was bad news if you were trying to spot a teddy-bear-suited elf on the lam.

But it worked both ways: The crowd also protected me from being spotted by him.

After buying a one-stop ticket, my cloaked form crept cautiously to the waiting InterRealm Express. It was an imposing black steam train decked out in white holiday lights. Adorning its front was a huge, seemingly indestructible Christmas wreath.

With an all-aboard warning whistle splitting my eardrums, I walked to the end of the train and showed my ticket to a uniformed walrus. He grunted and I climbed on.

I darted into the train's bathroom and locked the door. I'd decided to hide out in here until we started moving. I didn't want the elf to see me and escape before we'd even left the station.

Tired but determined eyes looked back at me in the bathroom mirror. Despite my overall lack of sleep, I felt energized and alert. With this much adrenaline coursing through my body, feeling tired wasn't even an option.

At last, after a series of whistles and jerks, the train gained momentum out of the station. With a deep breath, I exited the bathroom.

There was an elf outside impatiently tapping her foot. "Sorry, ma'am," I said, nodding sheepishly as I slipped past her.

Sneg was positioned at the front of the train, and I was in the back. Our plan was for each of us to work toward the middle, quickly scouring every train car until we found our target.

And we didn't have much time—the InterRealm Express was much faster than a typical commuter train. It would be a mere matter of minutes before we pulled into the BFF station.

Entering the first train car, I was greeted by the excited honks of a family of well-to-do snow geese. They were bundled up in winter clothes, their overhead compartments spilling over with presents.

Struggling to hear myself think, I walked through the aisle

and glanced between and behind seats—anywhere an elf might be hiding.

Using my claw to shield the mouthpiece from the honking noises, I squeezed a Pastel Pines Lodge walkie-talkie and said, "On board in the back, over."

Two seconds later, my walkie-talkie responded, "On board in front, eyes peeled and heading toward you."

The next car contained gnomes, fairies, nymphs, and imps from faraway forests and glens. Fairies zipped through the car, flitting playfully around my head as I searched for my target.

It would be very difficult for the elf to believably imper-sonate these creatures, so I kept moving, glancing between seats as I went.

I hoofed through packed train car after packed train car. I passed vampire coffins, leprechauns, a cyclops witch, and a group of rambunctious humans in the ugliest of ugly Christmas sweaters.

The next car up had a warning sign featuring a dung ball and stink lines. This car was designated for foul-smelling crea-tures to get their stink on in peace without disturbing other passengers. Many of the riders in this car were likely from Rancidia, the stinkiest country in the galaxy.

I plugged my nose, put my head down, and plowed through the car to get as little exposure as possible to the putrid odors within. Rushing through the car, I had to squint my eyes to protect them from the wafts of green stench that drifted lazily through the air.

When I emerged into the next car, I held my breath for as long as I could, hoping that the odors that had permeated my fur and clothing would have time to drift away.

I opened my eyes to find myself in the company of an otter, a muskrat, a beaver, and a porcupine. They were dressed in bulky winter clothes and listening to country music on a tinny-sounding speaker.

Satisfied this car didn't hide the elf, I headed off to the next train car. My walkie-talkie piped up, "Almost done with my half of the train, and no target sighted. How about you? Over."

"No target here," I responded. "I've cleared eight cars, including one awfully stinky—"

I froze in my tracks, and my eyes grew wide. A realization struck me as sharply as an icicle falling from the gutter: *I had no idea who was in the stinky car.* I had dashed through it so quickly with my nose plugged and eyes squinted, I didn't have a clue who was in there.

And if I were a devious elf trying to escape detection, surrounding myself with the world's stinkiest creatures wouldn't just help me avoid being noticed—it would actively repel anyone on the hunt.

I headed back to the stink car and put my claw on the door. Squeezing my walkie-talkie, I said, "Scratch that. I'm going back to the stinky car. The stinky car has not been cleared. Stand by. Over."

With the deepest breath I could muster, I plugged my nose and entered the car. After fanning away the green stench clouds, I saw a family of skunk apes, a trio of bog monsters, and a striped polecat.

I was running out of breath. I quickly breathed in through my mouth, taking in a heaping dose of the passengers' festering odor. It was awful. Compared to this train car, Ren's basement smelled like a warm tray of gingerbread cookies.

I had almost cleared every seat, when something made me pause at a karakoncolos couple.

The large creatures were covered in long, thick fur. They had so much fur, in fact, that it covered their faces entirely. They were something like Christmas sasquatches.

Their tray tables were down and they were hunched over, happily gorging on plates of rotten apples.

"Happy holidays," I spat out between shallow breaths. The

creatures continued munching noisily. The one closest to me offered a dismissive grunt.

"I hate to interrupt your lovely looking meal," I belted out quickly, "but do you mind leaning back for one second?"

The karakoncolos couple paused. Using apple-soaked paws, they parted their hair to peer at me with dark beady eyes.

In unison, they slowly leaned back to reveal a passenger tucked down by the window seat: It was a teddy bear band-leader wearing a gas mask.

"Bajazzo!" I yelled. "Or whatever your name is. You're coming with me."

I reached for the teddy bear's arm. Before I could grab him, he pawed a mound of rotten apples and flung it in my face. Gooey, rotten mush splatted into my eyes, nose, and mouth.

Frantically, I spat it out and wiped it from my eyes. By the time I recovered, the rotund gas-masked creature had scampered over seats and into the next train car.

I apologized to the karakoncolos couple and dashed away. They responded with half-interested grunts as I rushed out of the train car in pursuit of the jollifier.

"Suspect on the loose, Sneg," I said into the walkie-talkie as I barged into the next car. "Teddy bear on bottom and gas mask on top. He's headed your way."

The elf waddled past the woodland creatures. They stared

in awe, their twanging country music providing an ill-fitting soundtrack.

The elf turned back to look at me and lost sight of where he was going. His teddy-bear foot bumped into a banjo case, sending him sprawling onto the floor. When he hit the ground, his gas mask popped off his head and tumbled into the corner.

On hands and knees, the dazed elf shook his head. Without the golden wig covering it up, his hair blazed a fiery red. Despite the new hair color and teddy bear body, I could confirm without a doubt that this was our former client.

"Who are you?" I asked, taking a step toward him. "And why are you doing this?"

"I've been watching you since you were adopted!" cried the elf, staggering up from the ground. "And you don't even know who I am!"

Frantically, I tried to find this elf's face in my memory bank, but came up empty. *Who was he?*

He turned from me and waddled toward the train car door. He reached for the handle, but the door swung open from the other side before he could touch it.

The woodland creatures gasped, and the elf jumped straight into the air with a squeal. In the doorway stood a menacing, toothy-grinned krampus with claws outstretched.

"You've been very naughty this year, little elf!" The

krampus's voice was much higher than one might expect from such an imposing creature.

The elf formerly known as Bajazzo turned to me with burning hatred in his eyes. He was boxed in by krampuses in both directions.

Like a caged animal, the elf was sizing me up, trying to decide whether he could plow over me. Then, he stuck out his tongue and opened the nearby window.

Wailing winds washed into the train car as the elf laughed hysterically. It was an out-of-control, nothing-to-lose kind of laugh that I had heard once before.

In a flash, the elf clambered out the window and onto the roof.

I dashed to the open window and stuck my head out. The freezing wind screeched past as icy particles spiked into my face.

Fake krampus claws pulled me back into the train. "Don't do it, Ruprecht," said Sneg. "It's too risky."

"It's OK, Sneg," I said, looking into her yellow krampus eyes. "I grew up at the Christmas Castle. Riding on trains was a big part of my childhood."

What I didn't mention was that I grew up with *toy* trains. I was hoping that experience could transfer to the real thing.

Sneg's krampus head nodded slowly. "Fine, but please be careful up there."

I jumped onto the window ledge and clawed myself onto the train's roof. Once there, I rose up slowly on my hooves in a crouching position.

The teddy-bear-suited elf hadn't made much progress. He was crawling toward the front of the train on hands and knees, the tassels on his bandleader outfit blowing wildly in the winter wind.

I tested my hooves on the shiny metal roof and, leaning into the wind, began walking slowly, carefully toward my target.

The scenery rocketing past us was growing increasingly urban. By the looks of it, we would be nearing the BFF stop at any minute.

The elf reached the end of the train car and paused at the three-foot gap between him and the next one. He looked back at me with uncertainty.

"Stop!" I yelled into the wind. "We're not letting you get away with this!"

The elf rolled his eyes, his red hair whipping frantically in the wind. He turned back toward the gap.

Taking three steps backward, he padded forward and leaped across. He made it to the next car, but he fumbled the landing.

His furry teddy bear foot slipped on the metallic surface— he now slid helplessly toward the side of the train.

"No!" I yelled. No matter what this elf had done, I didn't

want to see him end like this.

At the last moment, the teddy bear suit provided enough friction to stop the elf from slipping off the edge of the train. He stood up slowly, momentarily startled.

Then the whistling train snapped him out of it. He whooped with victory as we pulled into the station with the gap between us.

On the right side stretched an outdoor train platform with large staircases leading down to Santa Claus Lane. To our left, a platform connected to BFF's entrance. Through the mall's glass doors and windows, I could see that it was already crawling with early-rising Christmas shoppers.

The elf crouched down to jump off on the street side of the train. But, for our plan to work, we needed him to enter the mall, instead of disappearing on the streets of Tinseltown.

And that's what friends are for. Before the elf could jump, a vengeful spirit appeared out of nowhere to block him from the city.

"Back, elf! Do as I say!" Marley wailed. Her arms were stretched wide, her hair blowing furiously. She had morphed her eyes into fiery orbs and contorted her mouth into an unnaturally fierce grimace.

It was terrifying, but it wasn't working.

Instead of screaming, the elf just laughed. "Ha ha ha! You

don't scare me! I was only pretending to be afraid of ghosts. That was an act, and you fell for it."

"That's fine," said Marley, returning to normal. "But how do you feel about giant cats? I believe you two are acquainted."

The elf's laughter broke off abruptly as an enormous, stealthy white cloud leaped down from a nearby building onto the city-side train platform. Train passengers screamed and darted away to make room for Jóla. She was crouched in a hunting position with backside wiggling dangerously, as if ready to pounce.

Not waiting to see what the cat had in mind, the elf ran off the other side of the train, rolled onto the ground, and darted to the shopping mall's entrance.

I lowered myself down from the train, ran into the mall, and tried to keep an eye on the elf as I dodged my way through a bustling throng of shoppers.

Up ahead, I could see the elf jump down one of the many twisting candy-striped slides that transport shoppers to the mall's lower floors.

I slid down after him and ended up crashing into a large ball pit. Knocking red, white, and green plastic balls out of my way, I struggled to the end of the shallow pool.

The mall was four stories of bustling shops, holiday lights, food stands, and giddy shoppers. Enormous ornaments, gift boxes, and electric reindeer hung from thick wires a hundred feet above the first-floor shoppers.

Despite the hubbub, the elf's blazing red hair helped me track him as he zigged and zagged through the crowd. He was heading in the opposite direction of the Christmas tree courtyard. I needed to change that.

There was a scooter store up ahead. I ran inside, threw a clawful of chestnuts on the counter—way more than enough, and courtesy of the elf I was chasing—and jumped on a cranberry-red electric scooter.

The elf clerk said, "Thanks for the tip," as I zipped out into the aisle and after my target.

Swerving around the smattering of shoppers, I quickly gained on him. He turned his head and his eyes got big as he spotted me approaching on his left.

My goal was to corral him to the right, and he hastily took the bait—he was now scampering toward the mall's main courtyard and the glorious multicolored BFF Christmas tree.

I slowed down and ditched the scooter. Marley joined me as we casually entered the courtyard together.

We saw it coming before the elf did.

As he scampered through the crowd, two majestic reindeer slowly descended from the second floor on the other side of the courtyard. But these weren't decorations. And they weren't alone.

Each reindeer had a passenger on its back. It was my parents, Santa Claus and Frau Perchta. They were dressed in their most resplendent red-velvet white-trimmed Christmas outfits. They were glowing with a golden aura of holiday magic.

In a booming voice, my dad bellowed, "Merry Christmas to all!" and my mom laughed, "Ho! Ho! Ho!"

Gasps and hushed whispers spread through the shoppers and mall workers. They all stopped immediately to gawk upward.

Some of the elves in the crowd shielded their eyes as the preliminary symptoms of jollification took hold. One of them ran away giggling with uncontrollable glee. Another pulled out a paper bag and began breathing into it with steady, deliberate heaves.

Two more reindeer floated down, each carrying three proud-looking North Pole elves in lively green outfits and triangular hats. They were my brothers and sisters: Annike, Brunhilda, Elias, Elke, Fritz, and Otto.

My smile was almost as big as the Christmas tree and the heaping toy sacks they landed beside.

Among the awestruck crowd was a guilty and terrified elf with nowhere to go. He dropped down to the ground to hide among the motionless horde, but it was too late. There was nothing he could do as the crowd parted to make way for my parents, the stars of the season.

As they approached the elf, they oozed confidence, charisma, power, and wisdom. Try as I might, it was hard not to feel a little starstruck myself.

CHAPTER FOURTEEN

KRAMPUS JUSTICE

Shoppers squealed and pointed as my parents made their way to the cowering elf.

My brothers and sisters skipped around distributing small baggies of coal to any elves who looked to be feeling the woozies of jollification. While North Pole elves were accustomed to beholding my parents, Townies and tourist elves didn't have the tolerance.

And my parents did look splendid. There was my mom in her lush red robe, holding her staff, every inch exuding her status as the world's most powerful winter witch.

And my dad had never looked more captivating with his voluminous snow-white beard, red-velvet suit, scuffed-up black boots, and a hat so iconic it was named after him.

The enormous reindeer lay like noble sphinxes near the tree: Dasher with his head of magnificent antlers, Comet with her beautiful black-speckled coat, Dancer with his pale pink undertones, and Cupid with her piebald pattern and curled bangs.

Everyone's attention was so transfixed by my parents and the magical reindeer that no one seemed to notice Jóla walking nimbly through the crowd, avoiding shoppers and proudly joining the reindeer.

In the middle of the parted crowd, I met my parents over the trembling teddy bear body. He was covering his head and muttering to himself.

"Thanks for taking a break from the grind, Dad. I know you have a lot on your plate." I walked between my parents and put one arm around each of them.

Concern cast a shadow over my dad's face. Thankfully, that was a rare sight. "I'm proud of you, Ruprecht. But I wish you hadn't taken on so much over your winter break."

"I know, Dad," I said. "Luckily, I had a clever ghost, a winter witch, and a giant cat on my side through it all."

"I can't believe you caught the jollifier!" It was my sister Brunhilda, joining us with all of my siblings. "Way to go, bro!"

"Seriously, nice work," said my brother Fritz. "You're going to be on the front page of the *Herald* for sure."

I group-hugged my brothers and sisters, and then, risking death, I even patted Jóla's white fur. "Merry Christmas, Jóla," I said. She responded with a short ground-quaking purr.

"Move it! Clear a path!" The familiar yeti bellow of Detective Metoh roared across the mall. He and Sergeant Schnee marched authoritatively through the crowd.

They reached us with a group of TTPD cops trailing closely behind. The elf cops among them tried their best to avoid looking directly at my parents. One had her hands on her knees and took deep, steadying breaths. The others pushed the onlookers back and began taping them off.

"Mr. Claus. Frau Perchta." The yeti greeted my parents, his fedora in his paws. Then he looked at me and Marley and dropped the courteous tone. "Ruprecht. Marley."

Schnee's brow was knitted with peeved wrinkles. "It's four days until Christmas, there's a jollifier on the loose, and we have no time to lose." She tapped the teddy bear costume with her foot. "So, what are we doing here, and who's the bear?"

With a deep breath, I turned toward the crowd. "This is your jollifier," I announced, as loudly and confidently as I could. "Nowell Rook, a.k.a. Bajazzo, a.k.a. whatever his real name is. He stole the snow globe from the Christmas Castle and used it to jollify elves in an attempt to frame me."

The ice troll scoffed. "OK, kid. As if we're going to buy that this has been an elaborate attempt to frame a twelve-year-old."

I knelt down to make sure the elf could hear me. "Ready to spill those jelly beans of yours, buddy?"

Still covering his head, the elf adjusted his arms so that his mouth was exposed. He yelled out, "It's a lie! I'm just a normal harmless elf! The krampus is behind this. The media and all the eyewitnesses say so!"

Metoh and Schnee exchanged a look. "He's right about one thing," said Metoh with a shrug. "Even if we wanted to believe Ruprecht's story, it doesn't change the fact that every witness describes a krampus as the jollifier, the third jollification was on Marley's doorstep, and Ruprecht fled the scene."

"It's true," I said, raising my voice to drown out murmurs from the crowd. "I did flee the scene."

I made eye contact with those in the front row. Most gave me their rapt attention, including Bock, Mari, and Mr. Marley. Among them was a shrouded older woman with white hair and a cane who looked back at me with disgust. Assuming she was not a fan of my species, I decided to ignore her.

"I fled, but only because I had to," I declared. "I had one chance to find the jollifier, and that's exactly what I did. It's only because I fled that I can now back myself up with evidence and witnesses."

My mom placed her hand on my shoulder. "Before you go any further, I invited a special guest who is very interested in what you have to say."

Raising her hand, my mom loudly declared, "Governor Lucia, please join us."

Warm golden light glowed from the mall's second floor. A tall woman with long, wavy blond hair and caramel skin descended on the escalator. On her head she wore a wreath crown of nine slender flaming candles. She was dressed in a white robe tied at her waist with golden rope. Even from this distance, I could see that her eyes were aggressively blue.

The crowd oohed and aahed at her majestic descent. The head of the Yuletopia government, Lucia was one of the most revered and powerful figures in the country. Several elves, just now recovering from the onset of jollification, were sent back into panic mode.

"I can't take it!" cried one elf as he scampered away, arms

flailing wildly in the air.

Governor Lucia arrived beside the naughty elf and knelt down to inspect his face. She turned her gaze up toward me and my eyes grew wide.

"Hello, Ruprecht," she said, standing up and shaking my claw. "It's not a smart idea to flee a jollification scene, nor should you ever withhold information from the police. But we can talk about that later. Right now, I'd like to hear the evidence your mom tells me you have uncovered."

"Thank you, Governor," I said, taking a bow. I wasn't sure if bowing was an appropriate thing to do in front of a governor, but I figured it couldn't hurt. "We'd be happy to tell you about our evidence, and show you as well."

Marley nodded and blinked out of sight as surprised noises sounded from the crowd. Shoppers were clearing the way for a large krampus, walking jerkily toward us.

"Everyone," I said. "I would like you to meet the manager of hospitality at the Pastel Pines Lodge. Her name is Snegurka."

Sneg removed her krampus head and waved to the crowd. She directed a formal curtsy to Governor Lucia and then to my parents.

"What is this, Halloween?" scoffed Schnee.

"This is the outfit the jollifier wore to impersonate a krampus," I said. "As Sneg is demonstrating, the costume is perfectly built to fit an elf."

"So what? It could have come from anywhere," said the naughty elf, still cowering pathetically on the ground. "It doesn't prove anything."

"Oh, don't worry," I said with a smile. "That's where our witnesses come in."

Ren the reindeer crouched under the police tape to join us. Two elf cops tried to stop him, but Governor Lucia waved them away.

"The krampus kid is telling the truth," he said. He pointed to the elf on the ground. "That elf bought the costumes and smoke bombs from my shop before all of this happened. He also used my storage services to stash the costumes and evidence, and he used my building's access to the sewer tunnels to sneak around."

Sneg raised her krampus claws in the air. "And I found this krampus costume and the tree-elf costume at his room in the Pastel Pines Lodge. That's where the elf duped his tourist victims, got them worked up about the snow globe, and then arranged the meetups in Tinseltown."

"But that's not all!" declared a disembodied voice as a burlap sack floated through the air above the crowd. The sack slumped down in a pile beside Lucia, causing the crowd to gasp.

There was a confused silence, and then Marley's form

materialized beside the pile. "Oops, sorry," she said. "I forgot I was invisible."

"And what do we have here?" asked Lucia.

"We have all the evidence you could ask for!" declared Marley, forefinger in the air.

She laid everything out on the ground. "Here's the tree elf costume and wig the elf wore to impersonate a ponderosa elf. Here's a business card to Ren's shop we found wrapped with a fruitcake, complete with the storage locker combination on the back. Here's the air fresheners he wore to smell like a ponderosa tree. And here's the miner's hat he used to creep through the sewers."

My dad picked up the miner's hat and examined it thoughtfully. "I know this hat," he grumbled, as if to himself. "The chimney sweeps at the castle wear hats like this."

"Wait a minute…" he said, crouching down to peer at the elf. The elf struggled feebly as my dad made gentle attempts to move his arms away from his face. Without much trouble, my dad held the elf up and examined him. The elf kept his eyes clamped tight, as if we wouldn't be able to see

him if he didn't see us.

"Hans?" said my sister Annike, bewildered. "The chimney sweep?"

"Yes, Annike, you're absolutely right." My dad's tone dripped with dark disappointment. "This is Hans von Trapp, a former Christmas Castle chimney sweep. At first, he was unrecognizable without soot covering his face. He's all cleaned up now, but that's him all right."

My dad set the elf down and turned to my mom and Governor Lucia. "I had to fire him several months ago for stealing candy canes."

"Yes, it's me, Santa," scowled the elf, dropping the scared act entirely.

"Wait a minute," I said. "You lied about being an expert thief, but in reality, you were fired from the Christmas Castle for stealing candy canes?"

The elf turned to me, face snarled with anger. Now that he wasn't pretending to be a timid elf from a faraway tree, this elf was seriously frightening.

"I only stole those candy canes so Santa would think his so-called *son* did it." He used his little elf fingers to put air quotes on the word "son."

"From the beginning, everything I've told you has been a lie," he seethed. "But you were too trusting and gullible to know better. I'm amazed someone so foolish was able to track me down. How did you do it?"

"First of all, Hans, you should try to be less sloppy about leaving clues everywhere you go," I said, breathing deeply to steady my nerves. "And secondly, I had a lot of help along the way."

Hans von Trapp, the former chimney sweep, turned his glare toward Ren. "Thanks a lot, you red-nosed faker." Then he turned his attention to Sneg. "And thanks to you too, traitor. Elves need to stick together so freaks like him don't take over Yuletopia."

"You stop right there," said my mom with a tone that meant business. "You've done and said quite enough. I think it's time justice was served, you naughty little elf."

"Naughty? Me?" The elf was furious. He pointed frantically at me. "He's the naughty one! All krampuses are naughty. It's who they are! They don't belong among polite elf society. I've been trying to prove it for years! Ever since you adopted this beast and brought him to the North Pole, I've been trying to prove it. I've tried to frame him with stolen cookies, fallen icicles, unwrapped presents—but none of it stuck. I even released a poltergeist at the Christmas pageant, and not even that could make you fools see him for what he really is—a nasty, naughty beast."

Schnee shot me a confused look. My heart swelled with redemption. Suddenly, my childhood took on a completely new meaning. It turned out I really did have a shadow of bad luck following me. And that shadow's name was Hans von Trapp.

"When Santa fired me, I vowed revenge," sneered the elf. "I couldn't believe he would kick me out of the Christmas Castle and allow this hooved monster to continue living there, tainting the place with his horns and claws and grotesque tongue. When the krampus decided to stay in Tinseltown for winter break without his parents around, I knew it was my chance to get him thrown in the Cooler for good. So what if a few elves had to get jollified along the way? Sometimes progress has its price."

"Prejudice is not progress, Hans," said Governor Lucia. "Your despicable actions come from a place of ignorance and hatred that have no place in our country. As the governor of Yuletopia, I hereby arrest you to await trial. In the meantime, you'll be the one spending time in the Cooler."

"You heard her, Schnee," said Metoh as he took a lumbering step toward the elf. "Let's book this creep."

"Actually," said my dad with a sly smile, "I had a different escort in mind."

He reached into his toy sack and pulled out a dingy black bell. It seemed very old, with strange inscriptions all around it.

My dad clanked it three times, and whispers swept across the crowd.

A strong whiff of sulfur emanated from the other side of the Christmas tree. For the first time, I noticed that all the lights on that half of the tree were out. Had it always been like that? Then I noticed that a full section of the mall was covered in shadow.

There was the faint sound of jingling bells. Then, from the shadows, came the thundering clop of one mighty hoof, and then another.

The entire mall seemed to quake as the biggest, hairiest, scariest, most ancient-looking krampus I had ever seen stepped out from the darkness.

He towered above all of us, even Lucia. His body was covered in charcoal fur, like mine. Wisps of smoke drifted up and off of his shoulders. Enormous horns sprung up from his head and curved to the side. Around his waist he wore discolored metal bells, and on his back he carried a large basket with several birch branches within. His expression was not angry, but of intense and unbreakable focus.

The crowd shrieked. Some hit the ground, some scampered away. Most, like me, couldn't take their eyes off this massive Christmas beast.

The krampus sniffed the air as nearby shoppers dashed away.

He emitted a grumble so deep it made my organs jiggle. Then he turned his scorching yellow eyes on his target: the naughty elf, Hans von Trapp.

The elf squealed and tried to flee, but Metoh grabbed him by the scruff of the neck and held him in place.

The krampus stomped toward us and stopped. He stood to my left. I looked up at him and then over to Lucia, who stood to my right. There I was, smack in the middle of the brightest and darkest shades of Christmas.

The krampus looked at my dad and nodded. My dad chuckled and nodded back. "Merry Christmas, Klaubauf," he said. The large krampus grunted. Then my dad turned to me, and so did the krampus. I gulped.

"Klaubauf, I'd like you to meet my son, Ruprecht," he said. The krampus grunted again and gave me a slight nod.

"Y-you know each other?" I asked.

"Yes, Ruprecht," said my mom. "Your father, Klaubauf, and I were good friends long ago. We still are, even though we've drifted apart."

I'd always thought my parents were pretty cool, but never more so than right now.

My mom motioned toward the diverse faces in the crowd, all beholding us with awe. "Krampuses and non-elf citizens like Bock, Mari, the Marleys, and even gremlins and goblins

have always been an important aspect of the holidays. Societies require a balance—elves are wonderful creatures, but they need a counterpoint. Otherwise, the North Pole, Tinseltown, and the holiday season would be far too sugary for its own good."

My dad walked over, pulled a photograph from his pocket, and handed it to me.

It was a sepia-toned and scratched-up picture of my mom looking much more like a forest witch than the Christmas witch I'd known my whole life. My dad was wearing a white robe with a weird tall hat and held a long scepter and a golden book. Between them stood the very same krampus that stood before me now.

They were all in front of my dad's first toy workshop that he and I had recreated for the snow globe.

I flipped the photo over. In old-fashioned cursive writing, someone had written, "Frau Perchta, Nikolas, and Klaubauf."

"This was soon after I'd met your mother," my dad said. "Back then, I went by Nikolas. And, as you can see, the fashion was a little different in those days. I had always intended to give this photograph to you on your twelfth Christmas. It turns out the timing couldn't be better. Merry Christmas, Son."

My heart fluttered as my eyes soaked in the photo. My parents looked ready to save the universe, and Klaubauf looked ready to eat a full village of children.

I just had to ask. "Did Klaubauf steal children when you were friends? Does he now?" I looked up at the beast. His eyes remained locked onto a whimpering Hans von Trapp.

My dad chuckled softly. "Things were tougher when that photo was taken. But even then, krampuses were more about scaring children with the threat of being carried away than actually going through with it."

The big krampus responded with a grunt and a slight shrug.

"We both always had the same intention," my dad continued. "We wanted to motivate children to act with kindness, empathy, and generosity. But, well, let's just say Klaubauf and I approached things with different motivational styles."

Governor Lucia raised both of her arms in the air to get the attention of the thunderstruck crowd.

"We haven't allowed Krampus Justice in this town for many, many years," she declared. "But it is still technically in our legal code. This naughty elf was going after a krampus. For that reason, I'll allow Klaubauf to serve as Hans von Trapp's official Yuletopian escort to the Cooler."

She raised a finger and sternly addressed the krampus. And, unlike the vast majority of us, she wasn't scared in the least.

"But," she said, with the voice worthy of Tinseltown's most powerful authority, "you must promise you'll only scare him. No torturing, no thrashing, no chains, or any of that old-timey stuff. And no dilly-dallying—take him to the Cooler without any detours."

Klaubauf considered it for a moment and then nodded in agreement.

Schnee put her icy hand on her forehead and shook her head. "Unbelievable," she muttered.

Hans von Trapp screamed as the krampus lurched toward him, picked him up like a sack of hazelnuts, and dropped him in the basket among the birch branches.

The elf continued to howl from within the basket, but his voice sounded distorted, as if he was blubbering from another, much scarier dimension.

Lucia leaned down and whispered in my ear, "That elf will be too scared to be anything but nice for a very long time."

Klaubauf heard what she said and grunted a deep, growling kind of laughter.

Part of me wanted to cheer, but that felt inappropriate. Instead, I just mouthed the word "Wow" to Marley. She replied by mouthing back the words "I know, right?"

Slowly, deliberately, Klaubauf clomped behind the dark side of the Christmas tree and let the shadows consume him. The cries of the hysterical elf faded off into the distance.

Then, in a snap, the lights popped back on, the shadows were gone, and the smell of sulfur was removed from the air.

CHAPTER FIFTEEN

LITTLE KRAMPUSES
EVERYWHERE

We did it. Marley and I solved our case, and the guilty jollifier was going to trial. The fact that he was being escorted by a powerful krampus was just a beautiful bow atop an already incredible Christmas gift.

My urge to gloat or dance or toast a mug of cider was quickly dampened when I remembered there was another part of our plan that hadn't worked out. Regardless of this success, our mission was incomplete.

I pulled the snow globe out of my satchel and gazed down at it.

"Great job, partner," said Marley, putting her arm around

me and sending electric tingles down my back. "One case and one solved mystery. The Krampus and Marley detective agency has a flawless record."

"You both deserve a great deal of credit," said my mom. "But let's consider putting a pause on the detective stuff when school starts back up."

"That seems fair enough," I said, and then to Marley I added, "Spring break isn't too far away."

My siblings came over for hugs and congratulations. I hugged each of them with one arm, as my other clutched the snow globe.

"That was so cool, Ruprecht," said Elke. She gestured to the heaping velvet sacks beside Dasher, Comet, Dancer, and Cupid. "But why did you ask us to bring these toys?"

"I thought someone else would show up," I said, scanning the crowd. "But I guess not."

Most of the crowd hadn't moved. Some, it seemed, hadn't so much as blinked since the action started. They were still gaping in awe at my parents and Lucia. Their original reasons for coming to the mall had been replaced by the desire to bask in the glow of these national icons.

It seemed that the glowering elderly woman was the only one not under their spell. Instead of gazing fondly at my parents, she was glaring irritably at me. Clearly, this woman had a thing with krampuses. I guess you can't please everyone.

"Did you invite our other special guest, Mom?" I asked. "I thought for sure she would arrive."

"Yes," said my mom. She had noticed the elderly woman too. "I sent my most trusted bluebird with a note." And then, with a slightly raised voice, she said, "I guess Grýla is too scared to show up with me, Lucia, and your dad here."

"Ha!" The elderly woman dashed toward me with shocking speed. "I'm not afraid of you do-gooder fools!"

She charged into me and tried to wrestle the snow globe out of my claws. I was able to clutch it against my body, but the struggle sent me flying backward onto the ground.

The stunned crowd took a step back.

"Hello, Grýla," said my mom, moving between me and the old woman. She positioned her staff diagonally across her body. "You received my invitation—how nice of you to join us."

The old woman held up her cane and crowed with evil delight. Her wicked laughter sent convulsing ripples of energy through her body, from her head to her feet, that transformed her into her actual form: Grýla the witch.

She held the cane high. It glowed with piercing purple light, morphed into the pentagram staff, and strobed thirteen times in rapid succession.

Shoppers yelped as Yule Kids rushed through the crowd,

pinching noses, knocking off hats, and flinging shopping bags into the air. When they arrived beside their leader, the shadows combined into a churning funnel cloud to await instruction.

Jóla hissed, and my mom stepped toward the tornado. She held her staff high in the air, ready to strike.

"The Yule Kids are the souls of once-naughty children!" my mom declared to the crowd. "Grýla has stolen them to do her dirty work, but they are not hers for the taking."

The top of my mom's staff glowed green and blue and purple. "Grýla—I'm giving you one chance to release these children."

Grýla responded with hooting laughter and a loud "Bah, humbug!"

The crowd gulped at the foul language.

"If this filthy monster doesn't fork over the globe," she fumed, "I'll steal his  naughty rotten soul and make him the fourteenth Yule Kid!"

I walked up beside my mom, and she nodded with encouragement. "OK, Grýla," I said. "You can have the snow globe, but only because it's almost Christmas and I'm feeling charitable."

I gave the globe a shake, took a second to admire the

fluttering snow, and casually tossed it to the witch.

As the snow globe traveled through the air, Grýla's shriek was joined by a higher-pitched yelp coming from the crowd. It was Pickwick, holding his hand up to his mouth.

Frantically, Grýla tossed her staff aside to catch the globe. Marley swooped through the air, snagged the staff, and then whistled innocently as she and the staff faded out of visibility.

"You fool!" cried Grýla, cradling the snow globe like a newborn. "I would have turned you into a throw rug if you had broken this."

A wide-eyed Pickwick wandered trance-like from the crowd, hands outstretched toward the snow globe.

"Back off, goblin!" Grýla snapped. "This dingus is mine."

Pickwick gazed lovingly at the globe as if in a deep dream. "But it's so...valuable."

"You only *think* it's valuable because you've been sold a story of pure fiction," I said. "I hate to burst your greedy fever dreams of wealth and power, but that's just a normal snow globe. Check out the bottom."

With a sharply bent eyebrow, Grýla turned the globe over and read the child-scribbled name. The Yule Kids swirled beside her.

"Ruprecht?" she asked, baffled.

"Yep," I said. "I made that snow globe when I was six with

the help of my dad. Hans von Trapp stole it to jollify elves with a made-up yarn about it being my dad's first toy."

Pickwick erupted with a deep groan and collapsed onto the ground.

"Actually, my first toy was a wooden cat," said my dad with a shrug. "I thought that was common knowledge." Jóla purred proudly at the mention of a cat.

"This is worthless! What a waste of time." Grýla cocked her arm back and tossed the snow globe into the crowd.

My mom aimed her staff at the globe, catching it in midair with a bright beam of energy. She guided it back to me, and I carefully placed it in my satchel.

"It may not mean anything to you, Grýla," said my mom. "But that snow globe has deep value for our family. I guess you never cared much for old-fashioned things like friends and family and holiday traditions."

"No, Perchta," Grýla sneered. "It's a shame to see a fellow witch commit her life and her strength to a human toymaker and a bunch of silly rituals. We could rule this town if you weren't so misguided."

Grýla gestured toward the swirling cloud of Yule Kids. "Our army could be infinite, and our power unlimited."

"Power is worthless if it's not built on love and kindness," said my mom, calmly.

"Oh, save it," said Grýla. "I don't have time to sit here and listen to you preach about right and wrong, naughty and nice. I have better things to do."

Grýla held a fist up toward the Yule Kids. When nothing happened, she pulled her empty hand down and stared at it.

"Where is my staff?!" she screamed, lurching toward us. We took a step back. She was pointing at us, her eyes feverishly searching for her missing power source.

"You can look all you want, Grýla," said Marley. "But you won't find it. It's in my special hiding spot in the ghost dimension, far beyond the veil."

"And, unfortunately for your precious time," said my mom, "I'm going to force you to listen to what I have to say. You're much easier to handle when you're disarmed."

My mom pointed her staff at Grýla and shot out a ray of green energy that engulfed the witch entirely. Grýla was held motionless as the magic force danced, fizzled, and popped around her. Her expression was frozen with a clenched mouth and wide open eyes, as if she wanted nothing more than to cry out in protest.

Behind her, the Yule Kids continued swirling, but considerably slower than before. From the cloud came distant-sounding murmurs of worry and confusion. With their captor weakened, they seemed numbed with uncertainty.

"Now, that's much better," said my mom, her voice booming across the mall courtyard. "Today, the first official day of winter, is your last day in possession of this army of shadows. We will no longer allow you to steal the souls of naughty children and force them to do your bidding."

"That's right, Grýla," said my dad. "We all have the capacity to be naughty or nice, and we all deserve a second chance. In Yuletopia, we don't turn our backs on anyone—not even the naughtiest children. We reward and we motivate, and, when needed, we punish. But we never forsake."

"These kids were naughty once," I said, stepping between my parents. "Here and there, I've been naughty myself. Like me, these kids deserve another chance. It's true their one-time naughtiness left an opening for Grýla to steal their souls, but our kindness can reverse that spell."

The Yule Kids had slowed down completely, bobbing in the air with white eyes focused on me.

Grýla, restrained by my mom's magic, could only watch, her only movement coming from the panicked darting of her pupils.

I walked up to the floating Yule Kids and presented the snow globe to one of the shadows in front of the pack. "Merry Christmas," I said.

The shadow's white burning eyes looked at me and blinked

with confusion. The distant murmurs intensified with alarm. And maybe a touch of curiosity.

The figure's shadowy black hands reached out toward the snow globe. When I let go, the Yule Kid held the globe for a split second before bright white light burst from its eyes and covered its form. In a flash of blinding illumination, the shadow transformed into a seven-year-old human girl with braided pigtails and a green knitted winter hat.

"Thank you," she said, gazing at the snow globe, tears in her eyes. "I'm so sorry for being naughty. I shouldn't have blamed the broken sled on my brother."

"Don't mention it," I said. "No one deserves to exist as a shadow pawn for an evil witch. I'll take naughty over evil any day."

The little girl shook the snow globe and watched as snow flurried around the humble shed resting between two evergreen trees. "What is it?" she asked.

"It's the stuff that dreams are made of," I said.

She held the globe in one arm and wrapped the other around my waist.

I turned to my siblings and gave them a wink. "You're up, family. Time to do what you do best."

My brothers and sisters walked up to the bobbing swarm of Yule Kids and each of them in turn presented their gifts.

One by one, my siblings' heartfelt gestures of forgiveness and generosity liberated six Yule Kids from their shadowy limbo: a fox, an elf, a pixie, a snow boy, a human boy, and a tortoiseshell cat.

Six remaining Yule Kids floated anxiously before us. Without hesitating, Mari stepped forward from the crowd and removed the crown of holly from her bone-white head. Carefully, she handed it to a shadow that immediately transformed into a young moose.

Governor Lucia unclasped a radiant golden necklace, handed it to a shadow child, and watched it transform into a young troll, face plastered with shock. Lucia laughed kindly and brought the troll in for a hug.

My mom offered a Yule Kid the brilliant holly leaf brooch from her cloak. The shadow accepted the gift and morphed into a snapping turtle.

My dad, the world's most famous gift giver, pulled a silver reindeer bell from his pocket and presented it to a Yule Kid.

The shadow returned to her original form of a little witch in a pointy hat. As she tried to process the situation, her eyes darted excitedly between my dad and the bell. It was very different-looking from his krampus bell, but something told me it had extraordinary qualities nonetheless.

With two Yule Kids remaining, Metoh stepped forward and

offered up his fedora. A Yule Kid accepted the gift and was a snowy owl once again.

Schnee sighed and, with a slight frown, conjured a beautiful snowflake ornament by freezing moisture particles in the air. She delivered it to a Yule Kid who transformed into a wolf pup. Then she turned to me.

Startled, I took a step back.

"Listen, furball," she said, her mouth scrunched thoughtfully. "I'm sorry I was so hard on you. I was wrong about krampuses, and I was wrong about you."

"All is forgiven, Sergeant," I said. "This season is all about starting over, wiping the slate clean, and offering second chances. I'll pretend we just met."

Schnee reached her blue hand out, and I shook it. As we shook hands, an icy shiver crawled up my arm and down my spine. When Schnee winked at me, I realized that she had delivered that shiver on purpose.

Metoh walked over with a deep chuckle. He rubbed my head with his big paw.

"Good job, kid," he said. "And don't worry about Schnee— she pulls that trick on me all the time."

With her staff's beam still suspending Grýla, my mom handed the staff to my dad. She walked up to the cord of light, pinched it off like it was made of licorice, and handed the end of it to Governor Lucia. Now the bad witch could be floated to the Cooler like a parade balloon bobbing down Santa Claus Lane.

"Please see that Grýla confronts the full extent of the law," said my mom. "These children deserve justice, and I think Grýla could use some time in the Cooler to consider where she wants to take her life."

"Thank you, Perchta," said Lucia, her crown of candles burning brilliantly. "And thank you, Ruprecht. Your detective work has helped bring justice to Tinseltown, just in time for Christmas. You and Marley will make powerful detectives someday."

A feeling of pride bloomed through my chest. I felt it for myself and for my best friend, Marley. I smiled at her in an attempt to communicate my gratitude. Her return smile made it clear she got the message.

My dad, being my dad, knew all of the former Yule Kids instantly. While Metoh and Schnee got to work reuniting most of them with their families, my dad knew that two of the children, the human boy and human girl, were orphans—just like him, and just like me.

Santa Claus crouched down to make eye contact with the timid children. "How would you two like to live with me and Perchta at the North Pole?"

The children squealed with joy and hugged their new dad. He scooped them up in his arms and looked down with eyes twinkling at me and Marley.

"We sure could use some help at the castle right about now," he said. "Would you two like to join us? We can start with some cocoa in the library."

My dad winked at Marley at the mention of the library, and she could hardly contain herself.

"You know it, Mr. C!" she said, celebrating with a ghostly fist pump.

Before we headed out, I had one more invitation to make. I found Sneg handing over the krampus costume to the cops. She jumped and hugged me before I could say anything.

"We got him, Ruprecht!" she said. "That was better than any movie I've ever seen, and it was real life!"

"We couldn't have done it without you, Sneg," I said. "And while I don't know if I can offer you an adventure like that any time soon, I can offer you some cocoa at the Christmas Castle."

Sneg laughed. "You had me at cocoa, Ruprecht. I accept!"

My dad rode on Dasher, the children hitched a ride on Comet, my brothers and sisters split up between Dancer and Cupid, and I climbed on the back of my mom's broom with Marley and Sneg.

Together, we soared through the mall, out the exit, past

the train station, and into the icy air, high above Tinseltown.

As we sailed away, I looked down on a city filled with elves, yes, but also one filled with a vast diversity of creatures. Some of them were nice, some of them were naughty. But all of them deserved justice.

Even if actual krampuses were rare, as far as I was concerned, any creature in need of empathy and compassion could be an honorary krampus.

And I would make it my business to look out for them. To extend the kindness my parents had extended to me when they adopted me from an orphanage twelve years ago.

I was committed to fighting for all the little krampuses out there in the shadows, the ones lost in the margins who needed a louder voice. All the little krampuses just waiting for someone to reach out with a claw of goodwill.

Sharing a broom with a ghost, a witch, and a hotel hospitality manager, I stared down at the city.

What a great place to be, I thought, *and what an even better place to belong.*

"Be well, little misfits, and take care," I whispered into the howling winds. "And good luck little krampuses, everywhere."

ACKNOWLEDGMENTS

My deepest thanks to Andrea Reuter, Reneé Yama, and Derek Sullivan for helping me bring Tinseltown to life with your careful attention, guidance, and invaluable contributions. Thank you to Al Ridenour for his enlightening book, *The Krampus and the Old, Dark Christmas: Roots and Rebirth of the Folkloric Devil*, and to Dr. Emily Zarka for introducing me to the Yule Cat. Thank you to Ellie for your reinforcement through an unlikely year. And thank you to all the readers, parents, teachers, librarians, and booksellers who have embraced our growing *Hazy Fables* universe.

Head to hazydellpress.com for Hazy Dell Press titles for all ages, including *Hazy Fables #1: Hobgoblin and the Seven Stinkers of Rancidia* and *Hazy Fables #2: Zombie, Or Not to Be.*

Middle-Grade Books
Ages 8-12

Picture Books
Ages 5-9

Board Books
Ages 1-7

Flap Books
Ages 0-4

📖 FREE EDUCATION GUIDES

And visit **hazydellpress.com/education** to download free classroom education guides for *Krampus Confidential*, including a guide to characters and customs from European folklore.